PILAR

"Bitch, you work at a gas station anyway. Ol fake, wannabe exotic looking ass hoe. I bet if you take that makeup off, you'll look like the rest of these basic ass bitches," the ugly, gold yuck mouth nigga spat before I stared him away from the counter.

Resting bitch face. The face that I use when these bum ass niggas try to talk to me. None of these niggas know how to approach a bitch, so I treat them accordingly. I don't know why I just stare at them, but I do. I chuckled to myself as he hopped in his old ass, broke down Mustang. I don't give a damn about these niggas, never have, and never will. I guess you can thank my punk ass daddy, Prince Harrison, for that shit. I can count on both of my hands how many times I have actually interacted with him. He didn't live in Mount Olive anymore, and that I knew for sure. Last time someone told me about my 'twin,' he lived in Jackson, Mississippi. I actually don't think he ever lived in Mount Olive, though. One time, I ran into him by accident at the fucking grocery store, with one of his bitches of the week. Who the fuck runs into their fucking father on accident? Me, that's who. It was awkward, and the bitch he was with was like 'aww, heyyy Pilar, he talks about you all the time.' I was like, 'well, bitch, I don't know why because I don't talk to him at all.' As usual, he made a bunch of empty promises, and

1

I haven't seen or spoken to him since then, so there's that. To tell you the truth, I don't even know how many kids Prince Harrison has, but I know there is more than just me—another thing he won't be truthful about—but whatever.

Yuck mouth got part of my description right though, except it's not fake. People do say I look exotic, but I think I look like a fucking cat. I got wide, almond shaped green eyes. I have really thick, already shaped eyebrows. I don't have to get none of that threading or waxing shit done, like other bitches do. I have a medium, button shaped nose, and also medium size lips. I'm in between Kylie Jenner, before she got the lip fillers, but not quite as big as they are now. My skin tone is legit the color of that caramel you get from McDonald's, when they give you those little apple crisps. My super curly hair that gets on my nerves because it gets tangled easily, stops right in the middle of my breasts. When I actually have the nerves to sit still, I'll let Mercy, or Swan as she is called by her family, straighten it. When she straightens it, it stops right at the top of my ass, since I am only five feet five. I guess I can thank Prince Harrison's Swahili features for my 'exotic' look as everybody calls it. At least that nigga's good for something.

"Pilar Renee Harrison, what the fuck is wrong with you, chile? Why you stare at him like that? Bitch, I'm deeeaaadddd." My ghetto ass best friend Mercy laughed, stepping to the counter.

"Girl, fuck that nigga. He comes in here every fucking weekend, same time, speaking that same shit. I'm sick of him. He does not get a single word from me, not ever. I really wish he would give it up. I'm not into that gold mouth, thug shit. I told him that the first time he bopped

DATE DUE

SEP 0 6 2018			
HWS 2-22-19			

H   RT

&   VN

BIANCA

© 2017

Published by Royalty Publishing House

www.royaltypublishinghouse.com

ALL RIGHTS RESERVED

his Bruce Bruce looking ass up in here. Swan, you know I needs me a sophisticated nigga with an education. I refuse to date a nigga like Prince Harrison." I laughed but I was dead ass serious.

"Bitch, I'm dead at the fact that your little ass calls your daddy by his whole name every time you speak of him. That shit be having me weak as fuck. Anyways, where the fuck is your replacement, I'm trying to hit this new pool hall that's opening tonight?" Swan asked while twirling her fingers in her long, gold-blonde ass wig.

"I don't know, but she needs to hurry the fuck up before I leave this bitch unattended. Free gas, alcohol, and snacks for every-fucking-body. Real fucking talk." I laughed and rolled my neck.

Mercy Swantae Washington is my best friend. We have been best friends since elementary school. We went through middle and high school being best friends. We even went to Jackson State University and graduated together. On the outside looking at how we interact with each other, you would think that we are just alike; but truth is, we are as different as night and day, but it works for us and has never interfered with our relationship.

"There goes that McDonald's hash-brown shaped looking bitch right there," Swan said, looking Carleeah up and down as she walked in the door trying to get herself together.

I had to stifle my laugh so Swan wouldn't continue her roast session. My one little laugh would have given that bitch the go ahead to continue the roast, and I didn't want that to happen. I liked Lee, and she was funny and real as fuck. Anytime you can make me laugh, you good in my book. Swan saw us talking and laughing when she came to pick me up from work one day, and she made it her business to tell Lee that I only had one friend, which was her. It's safe to say that Lee and Swan do NOT get along, not even for me, and they both loved me. I hope I can change that one day.

She looked Swan up and down before she smiled and waved at me. She went and clocked in, then came back and hugged me.

"Sorry I'm late, P. My stupid ass boyfriend was late picking me up—"

"You need a new boyfriend then," Swan interrupted her.

"At least I have one." She rolled her eyes at Swan. "Anyways, he picked me up late. His car broke down right now, and he was out making runs and shit. You know I gots me a hood nigga, ayyyeeee."

"A broke ass hood nigga if he can't afford to buy a new car. Very unfortunate, but like you said, ayyyeeee," Swan jigged like she was dancing.

I was like a deer in headlights, because I was in between wanting to laugh and wanting to knock Swan's ass out for being disrespectful.

"Come again?" Lee said.

"Oh nothing, just congratulating you on being with a broke hood nigga. I bet he be in the streets all day, and ain't got shit to show for it, but anyways, carry on. P, I'll be in the car," she said and walked out the store, still twirling her blonde ass wig.

"I'm gon' hurt your little friend. Don't look at me like that Lari, you know that we will never be friends, but again, I'm sorry for being late. I ain't gon' promise I won't be late again, because you know me."

"Look, Lee, it's not a big deal that you were late. I could use the extra time anyway. You know money ain't too good around here to begin with. We gon' get us some good jobs one day. I didn't sit my ass at Jackson State University for four years for this shit. Something got to shake, but let me get out of here. I will see you tomorrow night," I said while walking out the door.

"'Bout time you brought your raggedy ass out of there. Your ass was almost 'bout to work another shift if you had stayed in there a minute longer. I ain't joking either," Swan said as she pulled out of the parking lot.

"Shut up, Swan, and you need to stop being so mean to Lee. I like her, and you would like her too if you got the chance to know her. Ain't nobody gon' take your place in my life, ol' jealous ass bitch."

"Yeaaaaa… it's a no for me, big dog. You the only friend I need and want, so… no. Hold this wheel while I roll this blunt, and you better keep the wheel straight. You make me drop my weed like you did last time and I'mma smack you."

"Shut the fuck up and drive, hoe. I got this." I laughed and grabbed the wheel, something we'd been doing since high school.

I didn't have a car just yet, but Swan's parents got her one for graduation. This was actually her third car. She got her older brother's hand me down car when she first started high school. That car broke down right before we went to college, so she got her mom's old car, and her mother got a new one. Since she graduated college and stayed on the Chancellor's list the whole time, her parents got her a brand-new, zero miles, Hyundai Genesis. Unlike Swan, I was nowhere near as spoiled as her. My life was… complex, to say the very least. As crazy as this is about to sound, Swan was the only person who balanced my life out, making me sane.

My mother…well, the person whose pussy I came out of named Cisco Salem Green, had me when she was just eighteen years old. Can you imagine being two hours old and being addicted to crack? I'm surprised I'm not handicapped or some shit. God really does work in mysterious ways, but since I was born addicted to crack, she had to go to jail for a little while, where she got clean, or so my grandmother thought. She got her name because my grandmother, Lenora, was a smoker and a drinker, up until the day I found her lifeless body slumped over at the kitchen table. You wouldn't be wrong if you guessed that she had a glass of Cisco in front of her, and a burning Salem in her hand. I would never define Cisco as a mother because she never was. By the time I was seven, I knew how to cut and cook crack and measure cocaine. I was skilled at it too, and I thought I was the shit. However, my third-grade teacher, Mrs. Armour didn't think that was an appropriate talent for a seven year old. That bitch had me taken away from Cisco… again, sending her to jail, this time for a longer sentence. I didn't see Cisco again until I was twelve.

That second time, Lenora had adopted me and made me legally hers. Lenora didn't do all that she could, and was a piss poor grandmother for the most part. Most of the time, I would be across town at Swan's house, and Lenora would think I was in my room sleep. I was a wild kid, but I never gave her any trouble, especially since she was the only person in our family that cared for me just a little…not much though. My family was fed up with Cisco before I was even born, which means they didn't give a damn about me.

Prince Harrison's uppity ass family didn't give two shits about me, or his other kids that I know of. Let them tell it, my mother was a crack hoe that trapped Prince Harrison for his money, but little did they know, their precious son snorted shit too, but he never graduated to a different drug. Mount Olive had a population of less than a thousand, and the streets talked. They couldn't be stupid enough to think that a beautiful ass sixteen year old would get hooked on crack by herself. Crack... crack though! The most that young kids got addicted to was weed, not no fucking crack, but they were too stupid to see that. His old ass took advantage of my mom. He should have gone to jail for statutory rape, but that's neither here nor there.

On my first day of high school, Cisco came over to the house begging Lenora for money because she needed it for rehab again. She swore that she was going to stay clean, but Lenora and I both knew that she was lying, and she slammed the door in her face. That would be the last time that I saw Cisco alive. I was sitting in my Advanced English class when I was called to the office. Lenora had come to check me out of school. When we made it to the house, she told me that Cisco had overdosed and died. Lenora and I didn't cry at all, not even at the funeral. Prince Harrison had the fucking nerve to show up and sit at the back with all black on, like he was legit mourning. I rolled my eyes at him when we walked out the funeral home. I felt bad because she never got a chance to change her life around for good, but either way, at least she was not suffering on this cruel earth anymore.

"Bitch, my hand finna fall off. You tryin to hit this shit or naw?"

Swan asked me, bringing me out my thoughts.

I snatched the blunt from her and took three long pulls before I handed it back to her. I was stressed out, and tired from that bum ass job at Love's. When Swan and I graduated from college, we wanted something different. I didn't want to move because of Lenora, but after I found her dead, I realized there was absolutely nothing in Mount Olive, Mississippi left for me, and that's when we chose Jacksonville, Florida. The good ol' Duval County. I thought that since this was one of the largest places in the United States I would have found a job easily, but I was wrong as shit. The only job I could find was Love's, so I had to roll with it until I found something more in my field. I got my degree in Health Science, and Swan got hers in Health Administration, so she found a job easily. I know they sound the same, but they are totally different. I was stressed because bills were coming in, and they were more than the money I was bringing home, especially since the $10,000 check Lenora left me was running low… extremely low.

"Stop worrying, Pilar. I told you that if you need me to pay a little more on the bills, then I will. You my bitch and my best fucking friend. I know you would do the same for me. I know you stressing out about not having a job in your field. You'll be alright. Let's go out to this pool hall, let your hair down, and don't think about that shit right now. I heard that it was supposed to be jumping. They been talking about it on the radio for the last couple of weeks."

"You're right, Swan. You're right."

Two hours later, we were dressed and ready to head downtown to this new pool hall that this bitch kept talking about. I don't know how to play pool, but I know more than playing pool is going to be going on. I put on a tiny blush pink dress that fit my curves perfectly. That's one thing that I'm thankful that I got from Cisco: my perfect perky 36C cup breasts, small waist, and a perky plump ass. I put on some skinny toe nude heels that I ordered from Fashion Nova a couple of weeks ago. Swan's ghetto ass put two puffballs at the top of my head and let the rest of my hair hang down, so I was looking like Mickey Mouse. She let me get one of her nude Chanel bags. I wouldn't dare buy anything that expensive, but she got a good job and can afford it, so more power to her.

Swan's sexy tall ass had on a brown strapless bustier that stopped right above her pierced belly button, and she had on a nude pencil skirt that accented her body perfectly, paired with a nude pair of spiked red bottoms. Swan was five feet ten, and had perfect, chocolate, blemish free skin. I mean this bitch's skin was perfect. She could be a model, but she didn't want to do any of that. She had taken her ghetto blonde wig off and put on a jet black one. She was the queen of slaying hair, makeup, and fashion. She was the reason that I could look fly as hell in a Walmart outfit. We were also literally night and day in looks as well, but we were both bad bitches.

When we pulled up to *Duke's Pool Hall*, the fucking line was around the corner. When we finally got in the damn building twenty minutes later, to my surprise, it was more than just playing pool. It was a bar, a lounge, pool tables, poker tables, slot machines, and girls walking around half naked serving shots and drinks. This looked a like a strip club, lounge, and casino all in one. This was going to make the perfect hang out spot, especially after the long day that I had. As soon as we sat down, we were interrupted by a fine ass man dressed down in a tailored suit. I didn't even mean to lick my lips, but I did, and he smirked at me.

"Hey, ladies, have a couple of shots on me. I'm the general manager of this place, Brandon Lewis. If you need anything, please don't hesitate to find me, especially you. What is your name?"

"My name is Pilar."

"Beautiful name for a very beautiful girl. Here is my card, please give me a call sometime. My direct number is on the back," he said and walked away.

"Are you going to call him?" Swan asked me.

"Hell no. Look at him over there probably giving the same line to those other bitches. I ain't stupid by a long shot child. He might be fuckable, but that's it. He ain't relationship material. You know Jacksonville is like third on the list for having the highest rate of HIV, and I love my clean pussy so that's out," I said while shaking my head and ripping up the card simultaneously.

"Bitch, I'm deaddddddd. Let's finish these drinks and dance, hoe. I didn't come here to sit down. I came to shake my thick assssss, ayyyyeee."

For the next couple of hours, we danced and drank more drinks. We didn't have not a care in the world. On the way out of Duke's, I bumped into Brandon again.

"Shorty, I can't wait to hear your voice on the phone," he smirked.

"I bet you can't, but don't hold your breath," I replied and kept walking.

"Bitchhh, I'm weeeeaakkkk. You don't care what you say," Swan said, laughing.

We pulled up to our condo on the beach an hour later. That's one thing that I would never get to use to; everything in Jacksonville being so spread out. Swan had to drag me out the car. I'm really not a drinker. I slept good that night, especially with the effects of the weed and the alcohol. I knew for sure that I was going to be hung over tomorrow.

BRANDON 'BLIZZY' LEWIS

*L*ast night was a fucking 'lit'uation. I honestly don't even remember how I got the fuck home, but I am surrounded by three sexy ass mothafuckas. I raised the covers, and we were all naked as the day we were born. There was like six condoms in the bed, so last night had to have been good as shit, and I'm so fucking pissed that I don't remember the shit. I guess I had wayyyy too much to drink. I moved their hair out of their faces, and was low-key kind of pissed that one of them was not the little Mickey Mouse chick that I remember for sure. She was one of the craziest looking chicks that I had ever seen. Although she was scary looking, she was sexy as hell. I know it's weird, but still. I looked at my phone and saw that I had no missed calls.

I'm a lil' tight that Mickey Mouse hadn't called me. She must be one of those, 'I'mma wait three days to call' types. It gotta be that, because ya boy ain't never had a problem getting chicks. I'm every woman's dream guy. My name is Brandon Lewis, but they call me Blizzy. My teammates gave me that name in high school when I played sports, because I could blitz by anybody and get a touchdown, or a dunk. I'm six feet five and weigh a little over 200 pounds. I'm slim, but a nigga is solid. The light skin, green eyes, and big ass pink lips, is what gets the girls, and also the fact that I wear a size 13 shoe. I can't speak for no other niggas, but the dick to shoe ratio is true for me. My twenty-eighth birthday was a few months ago.

"Damn, I don't even know these hoes' names," I whispered to myself as I scratched my head. "Aye, y'all get up. Y'all got to go," I said, and the one on the left started stirring.

"Blizzy, shut the fuck up. You in our house. If anything, you got to go."

I looked around again, and this bitch wasn't lying. She was right… this ain't my damn house. I got out the bed and went and emptied my bladder. I was still a little loopy from last night. I put on my t-shirt and slacks, and headed out. When I went out to my brand-new BMW, I checked my wallet to make sure all my cards were still in there. I had to make sure everything was still intact. I know how people do because I do the same shit. I am what these hoes call a scammer. I get what I want, how I want, and when I want it. I always use my good looks and good dick to my advantage. I got a house in a bitch's name, and I get a new car every other month in a bitch's name. All I have to do is whisper sweet nothings in their ear, and viola, I got a new bitch to finesse.

See, I know people be looking at me like I'm a fuck nigga for doing what I do, but it ain't my fucking fault. It's these low self-esteem bitches, fathers' fault. They didn't have a father in their lives, and now the first dude that whispers sweet nothings in their ear, they ready to give their all to them. So, they can't blame me for the shit. I ain't always been this way though. I had a promising future for real. I graduated from Ribault

High School and got a full-ride academic and athletic scholarship to University of Florida in Gainesville. I played for the Florida Gators as the quarterback. Hell, I threw the winning Hail Mary at the game that won us the fucking championship. My life was fucking perfect, but that perfect life ended the day this bitch had her stupid ass brother to 'Tonya Harding' me. If you ain't familiar with Tonya Harding, then long story short, she wanted to win an ice skating championship, so she 'allegedly' had someone to beat the other woman in the legs so she couldn't compete. So, yeah, that's what happened to me.

It was a month after I had graduated from college, and a week after I had been chosen number seventeen in the first-round draft pick to the Jacksonville Jaguars as a back-up quarterback when I got attacked. Man, I was on cloud nine, especially since I had been watching the Jaguars since I was a little boy. I was at the track, practicing on my sprints so I could be prepared for camp that was going to start a few weeks later. When I was on my way to my car, Cecilia, this bitch I was fucking with in college, was sitting on the hood of it. She told me that she was pregnant, and as soon as she told me that, I told her my future was too bright for a child, so she needed to get an abortion and if she didn't, then she would be a single parent. I didn't even know her brother was in the next car over and heard everything that I said to her. He got out the car with a lead pipe, and started beating me in my legs until he shattered both of my tibias. Before he jumped in the car and drove off, he told me that my NFL career was over. I never saw Cecilia again. I don't know if she got the abortion or not, so I could possibly have a child out in the world. After that brutal attack, no team wanted me because I was a liability, so my career was over before it started. At least that crazy mothafucka is going to spend the rest of his life in jail for doing that. I had a degree in Kinesiology, but I ain't want to do nothing with that. So, that's when Blizzy the finesser and scammer was born.

As soon as I walked in my house, my phone started ringing. I looked at the caller ID and it was Duke calling me.

"What up, my G?" I answered the phone.

"Blizz, what's going on, my man? I was calling you to make sure you were straight. You followed some fine bitches out the club last night."

"Yeah, man, I just got home. Shit, when I woke up this morning, I thought I was at home. It was jumping last night. What was the count, I know you made some money last night, nigga?"

"Man, it be like that sometimes. I'm at the office now, printing out the count. Hol' up. We had a packed house last night. I mean, we were at maximum capacity. This make me think that I should have gotten a bigger spot. What you think?"

"Let's see what the next couple of months look like first, and then we will see if we should look into getting a bigger building, but I need a favor from you."

"What's up?"

"Can you use your resources to find a Pilar? She was the little chick who came in with the light pink dress on last night. She was a very weird looking chick with puff balls on her head."

"Do you have a last name?"

"No, all I know is Pilar."

"Aight, bet," he said and hung up the phone.

I laughed at him trying to sound like us. I say us because Duke is Egyptian. I think that's what they are called. He'd been over here since he was like sixteen, or something he said, and it's crazy how strong his accent is at times. I guess it's because he didn't speak a lick of English when he moved here. I couldn't wait until he got back to me with Pilar's information, but in the meantime, I was going to scroll my little black book to see who I can finesse for these new Yeezy's that's about to drop next month. I might get Mickey Mouse to get those if she's on my bus of bitches by then.

BARAK 'DUKE' RAMSES

I couldn't believe how off the fucking charts last night was. It was nothing like my New Orleans turnout was, but it was definitely close. The building that I had in New Orleans could hold over 700 people, and the one I purchased here could hold only 500, but either way, I got paid. I have a pool hall in New Orleans, Miami, and now Jacksonville. Duke's is getting his name on the map, and I plan on adding a couple more before the year is out. I don't want to spread myself too thin though. Don't get me wrong, I love the traveling back and forth, but sometimes it can become too much. That's why I hired Blizzy to be my general manager for this location here. I met Blizzy back in 2006 when I moved here after I evacuated from New Orleans during Hurricane Katrina, and he seemed like a pretty cool dude. His only problem is that he can't handle his women, and sometimes it can interfere with business.

A little about me. I'm a hoe. Let me just put that out there. I'm a hoe, a big one, but my hoes wouldn't dare try that shit that they try with Bliz because I'll cut their ass off so fast their head will spin around twice. I probably shouldn't have said that first, because I'm sure you probably think differently about me and shit. I don't really give a fuck though. At least my bitches all know I'm a hoe, and don't try to make me settle down, because they would only end up getting their feelings hurt. I'm a sexy ass, dark chocolate ass nigga, and everything about me is big as fuck. I'm six feet five and 210 pounds. Big—my nose; big and wide—my eyes; big, unless I'm gone off some good ass weed—my ears; big—my lips; big—my dick… eleven inches long, six inches in girth… big. So, yeah, everything about me is big as hell, but after all of that shit, I swear I only get bitches because of my deep voice and accent to match it. Yeah, a nigga not even from around this bitch, and here I am making more money than these niggas ever seen in their life… legally. If I ain't about shit else, I'm about my mothafuckin' business. So when niggas, including my brothers, tell me that I stunt too fucking hard, I remind them niggas that we have every fucking right to, especially after everything we have fucking been through and accomplished together. We ain't always been these well accomplished ass niggas. Let me go a just a lil' deeper into my personal life.

I was born into royalty. Not like people who are born with a silver spoon in their mouth, I was actually born into royalty. My dad is the King of Egypt, and if you know a little bit about royalty, then you know since I'm the first-born son, I am in line to be the King. My name is Barak Ramses, but they call me Duke. My dad is also Barak Ramses, but they call him Dutch. I have four moms because my dad has four wives. You know in Egypt, they can do shit like that. Hell, you can also beat your wife or kill they ass with no penalties if you want to. Wait, not kill them for the fuck of it, but if they get disrespectful or shit like that. Over there in Egypt, we don't play that shit. Women are beneath us, and that is the fucking end of it. What we say goes, and it ain't no back talk. If a bitch backtalks my dad, they liable to get their neck snapped, and their mother will get a post card in the mail letting them know what happened…that's if he's feeling remorseful, something my dad barely felt. Well since he's the King, they respect him anyway. I'm supposed to be marrying my first wife, Edwina Dubar, when I turn thirty, and if I want more, then I can have more. That's not too long from now. Edwina is a fine ass, thick ass, yellow bone. We were each other's first on our sixteenth birthday, right before my dad dropped me and my brothers off in the States, so as he says, 'we could become men.'

The reason I stunt so mothafuckin' hard is because I fucking deserve to. At age sixteen, my dad dropped me and my younger brothers off in New Orleans and chucked the deuces at our asses. Baron was fourteen, Bakari was twelve, and Bomani was ten. It was my job to take care of them, and make a way for them. We couldn't speak a lick of English. Imagine trying to find an Arabic translator and having to have one everywhere you go; school, work, interviews. My dad only gave me five thousand American dollars to work with, so I had to make that shit work. I got us some place to stay, and got us four air mattresses. I had to make sure that my brothers got their asses up and went to school daily, and every night we would get on that Rosetta Stone. The only brother that gave me a little trouble was Bakari. That nigga didn't want to do shit. He thought that this shit was pointless, especially since Dutch was the King. He felt entitled, so me and him had to come to blows a few times so he could get his fucking mind right.

On my eighteenth birthday, I was feeling myself because I could finally speak fluent English. I was on track to graduate high school at the top of the class, and my brothers were on the honor roll. I went inside this pool hall to celebrate my birthday, and I met this nigga named Amp. He was the owner of the pool hall. He could tell that I wasn't from around there, so he took me under his wing, showing me the ropes of owning my own business. So, after I graduated high school, I went to college for business administration, and before I even graduated college, I had opened my own pool hall. Of course, Amp wasn't feeling that because he felt like he should be a silent partner, because he did show me the ropes of owning my own business. We were going to have a meeting, but right before the meeting we had to evacuate New Orleans, and honestly, that was the last time that I saw Amp. Some say he didn't evacuate and drowned, but I don't know. That nigga was smart.

I packed up what I could, and me and my little brothers came here to Duval County. They finished school here, and I got my Masters of Business Administration at University of North Florida. A year or so later, I reopened Dukes in New Orleans since I was more familiar with that place. A year after that, I opened one in Miami, and now here in Jacksonville. So yeah, when a nigga tells me I stunt too hard, I let them niggas know that I have a fucking reason to. I'm a self-made millionaire, without the help of my rich ass father. I fed three growing boys, and made sure they all got college educations. Well, Bomani will be graduating soon, but you get my point.

During those 'becoming a man' years, I spoke to my dad often, but never about coming home. I had to prove to that nigga that I deserved my fucking crown. My dad said that Grandpa Barak did the same thing to him, so it was only right that he did the same thing for me. Every two weeks, I'd fly home to beat Edwina's pussy up, visit my moms and dad, and then come back to the States. That's why I'm a hoe, because my wife to be will never find out, and even if she did, she wouldn't say shit because she knows what would happen to her.

I pulled up to my security gate, scanned my card, and went through. I live at Jax Beach on Ramses Avenue. Yeah, I bought a whole a fucking street and had my mansion built at the end of it. It was 30,000 square feet with a bedroom for every day of the week, an inside Olympic size pool, and a gym. Each of my brothers had their own house on our street, but their houses weren't as big as mine. Company comes through the front gate. Only my brothers know that it is an exit at the back of my house. When I entertain women, I don't bring them to my house. I have a loft downtown that I take them to. I definitely wouldn't step foot into their house where I'm vulnerable and shit. You never a know, a bitch might try to set a nigga up to be robbed or some shit like that. Don't think for one second that I don't know how to protect myself though. When I first got to the States, a nigga at school tried to play me, and I dislocated his jaw with one swing. He ain't fuck with me no more after that.

"Mariahhh, I'm here. What you got for me baby?" I asked my housekeeper and best friend, as I walked through the house.

"Yes, your majesty?" She appeared and curtsied.

"Ugghhh, when I hear 'your majesty' I think of my father. Please, please, please, call me Duke."

I told her that she didn't have to do that, but she does it anyway. I only needed one housekeeper since I'm the only one who lived here. She does pretty much everything for me. She is from my country. She wanted to come to the States and see what it was like. I don't know why though. I have been living here for almost half of my life, and I would still much rather live in my native country. Mariah is also my legit best friend. I say legit best friend because we have never done nothing pass hug or kiss on the cheek. You know nowadays, people call people they have fucked their best friend, and we have never done anything of the sort.

"What you cook for me today, baby girl?"

"I cooked you a loaded chicken gyro, and I have you a glass of Dom Perignon waiting for you on the table. How was the grand opening last night?"

"It was really packed as shit. You should have come. You were off last night," I said to her as I was sitting down at the table.

"Your..." I glared at her. "Mr. Duke, I should have come. I will come the next time that I am off."

"I'm going to hold you to that, Ms. Mariah."

I left out the room and went into my office to look for this girl's information for Blizz's ass. It's funny that he wants me to look for information. Like, he ain't never had a problem getting a woman before. He said her name was Pilar and she had on a pink dress. I scanned the cameras and I saw her. I got a good face recognition on her and it gave me Pilar Harrison, and she works at a gas station. Figures. Bad bitches always have dead end jobs. She might be trying to come up off a young boss. I called Blizz and gave him the information, and he could do whatever he wanted to do with it.

PILAR

I stretched out in my queen size bed, and jumped up when I caught a Charlie horse in my leg. I hobbled around the room until the cramp finally dissipated. My head was slightly hurting from last night's festivities. I had to be at work in a few hours, so I will just pop an Advil or two, and I will be just fine. I walked in the kitchen to see that Swan was in the living room doing yoga without me. You would think that Swan would be more of a calm person since she never skipped a day of it, but nah. This bitch is a hot head.

"Good morning, Swantae," I spoke, calling her by her middle name which she hated so much. She hated her first name even more, although I liked the name Mercy, and am probably going to name my first daughter after her; if I ever have kids, 'cause only God knows how bad my nerves are for noise, which includes excessive talking, smacking on food, chewing and popping gum loudly. So, yeah, I'll probably be about forty before I have kids, but by then I'll be going through menopause, so… I'll probably never have kids.

"Shut up, hoe. It's more like good afternoon, lightweight. This is why your ass needs to drink more. I swear I get sick of having to drag your ass in the house because you can't get out the damn car. You don't know how heavy your ass is. You little and all, but not that damn little," she said.

"Well thank you for carrying me in. That's what friends are for anyway. Don't act like I ain't drug your raggedy ass in here a couple of nights, and you big as fuck. So, there's that. Thank you for cooking me some breakfast," I said as I popped a piece of bacon in my mouth, and instantly spit it out.

"Wrong bacon, bitch."

Swan always eats healthy. She doesn't eat meat at all. I try to eat healthy sometimes, but the shit just does not work out for me. I work at a gas station, and all those snacks in there be calling my name like crazy.

"I find it so funny how a mothafucka don't eat meat, but finds every possible substitution for meat. Chile, I'mma trick your ass one day. Again, thanks for cooking breakfast for me."

"You don't have to thank me for that, but listen, there is a job that just came open for an Office Coordinator, if you want me to see if I can get you an interview for it. They are looking to fill the position rather quickly. If you say yes, then I can shoot my HR manager a text, and he will call you for an interview after you apply online. I'll make sure that you get the job. He owes me a favor anyway."

"First of all, bitch, I don't want you fucking nobody just to get a job for me. Is the job hard?" I asked.

"Bitch, it don't matter if the job is hard or not. That is why you sat your raggedy ass in school for four years, so you could do something that was in your field. It pays good, and you'll be able to turn in that damn bus pass. I can save my gas coming to pick your ass up late nights, and I don't have to pretend to be your girlfriend anymore, when those yuckies try to come talk to you." She started laughing.

"Blah, blah, blah. Okay, bitch. I'll take it."

"Okay, I knew you would. Just send over your resume and cover letter to this email address. Do it before you go to work. They will be calling people for interviews soon." She handed me a card.

I went back in my room and looked at the time. I had to be at work in a few hours, but the bus over here runs so fucking early that I sometimes be at work like an hour early. I was in the middle of sending over the resume and cover letter, when I got a video call from an unknown number. The good thing about having a MacBook is your phone can connect to your computer, and you can answer all your calls and texts on the computer, especially since my phone is on charge.

I answered the ringing from my laptop, and then clicked back on the screen I was working on. I kept typing for a few minutes, but I didn't hear anything but wind in the speakers, so I clicked back on the camera part.

"Hey, Pilar, how is my favorite daughter doing?"

"Prince Harrison," I spoke through gritted teeth.

This man gets on my nerves so bad, and I only talk to him every red moon. We are only going to talk for five minutes; well, he's going to ask questions and I'm going to answer them. He's going to say or ask me something ignorant, and I will probably curse his ass out and then hang up. After that, I probably won't talk to him until another red moon. That's pretty much how our relationship is.

"You don't have to call me by my whole name. Prince or Dad is just fine."

I just stared at him, because I know there is a reason that he is calling.

"So, I thought I told you to call me before you moved to Jacksonville."

"Prince Harrison, I'm sure someone told you that I was moving here. Mount Olive is small because I didn't tell you I was moving to begin with. That must was one of your other kids you were talking to."

He pinched the bridge of his nose before he responded. See, he gets irritated with me just as quick as I get irritated with him. I believe that is also part of the reason we don't get along. I got up from the computer and started pulling my work clothes out so I could iron them.

"You are my only daughter, Pilar. I don't know why you don't believe that. So, how's it going in Jacksonville? I have been there a few times. Where did you go? I can't see you anymore."

"Well, I have to get ready for work. That is what most normal people do, and not live off of different people."

"Well, I will let you go. You can save this number and use it sometimes."

I rolled my eyes towards the ceiling because Prince Harrison ain't never had the same number. When he does call, it's from a different number, and he tells me that same shit every time. I tell him I will save it and I will call him. It's same ol' song and dance that we do.

"Sure."

"Before I let you go, I was wondering if you wanted to make a few quick bucks. I know you are down there working at a gas station. I'm sure you need some money to pay off your student loans, and shit. Do you want to sell—"

"You have some fucking nerves. If the person that's running my business told you that I work at a gas station, that mothafucka should have also told you that I got a full ride to college and I don't have any student loans. Something you would know if you were to be in my life like a real father, versus only hitting me up when it benefits your ugly ass. Whatever you were about to ask me to sell, the answer is no. Goodbye, Prince Harrison," I snapped, and then hung up on him.

See, just as I predicted. He will never change, and I don't even know why I be expecting him to. I looked at the time and saw that I had already missed my bus. I knew Swan was going to be mad that she had to take me to work, and she was going to have to pick me up. I can't wait until I get my own car.

"Swannnnn," I sung her name as I tapped on her door.

"I'm coming, Pilar. I heard you in there fussing with your pappy. Your ass might have to call a cab to drop you off. I'm trying to get me some ding-a-ling tonight."

"From who?"

"Girl, our neighbor's husband. He got some sexy ass pink lips."

"He's white."

"He's got a dick. What the fuck him being white got to do with anything? That man likes to eat chocolate pussy from the back. I'm finally going to let him fuck tonight. Don't look at me like that. Your ass works a crazy ass schedule and I be bored. He was sitting outside one

29

day when I came home from my run on the beach. He flat out told me that he wanted to eat my pussy because he ain't never had chocolate pussy before. You think my ass was going to turn down free head? Absolutely not. That man had me nutting from left to right. Now come on, because I have to get a wax."

I shook my head at Swan because she was a fool. She dropped me off at work, and I made it just in time. Lee was there, and I hoped that she was working an extra shift, because I really didn't feel like being here by myself tonight. Normally when I work nights by myself, some of the truck drivers come in and keep me company. Since it's the weekend, the store is probably going to be jumping anyway.

"Heyyyy, Lari," Lee spoke, while waving at me.

She calls me that for short, even though I don't think that 'Lari' is short for Pilar, but whatever.

"Hey, girl. What's been going on? You worked a double shift or are you just now getting here?"

"No, bitch. I will be here with you tonight. So, catch me up on what happened last night. How was the little club thing you and your little friend went to last night?"

"It was aight. It was packed as shit though. Girl, I got drunk and high. It seems like a cool place to hang out at on the weekends, but I'm not sure how often I will go."

"What did you wear?"

I pulled out my phone and showed her a picture of me, and what I had on.

"Damn, Lari, I know you met some fine ass niggas last night. I keep telling you that I can put you up on one of my nigga's friends. They are all fine as shit."

"Girl, you know I told you I don't want no hood ass nigga. They can't do shit for me. I ain't the ride or die kind, because eventually you may have to die. So, that's a no for me."

"Hood niggas will change your fucking life. They will have you doing things that you thought that you would never do. Trust me."

"I don't want to do things that I don't think about doing. So, I'll pass."

I love working with Lee because she makes time go by so fast. Every other hour, we have to clean the bathrooms and make sure everything is stocked properly. I hated everything about working at a gas station, but some of the people that came through there were really nice. The women's bathroom was always the nastiest, which blew my fucking mind. Women are supposed to be the cleanest species, but they aren't. I came out of one stall, just when this little white woman and her daughter were coming in the bathroom.

"Let's not use this one, sweetie. She just came out of there," the woman told her daughter who was looking confused.

"What the fuck does that supposed to mean?" I asked her.

She started stuttering, because I guess she didn't think I was going to say something.

"Little girl, I hope while your mother is teaching you ignorant tactics, I also hope she is teaching you to squat over a gas station toilet, and to wipe from front to back," I said to her daughter.

I left out the bathroom because she had pissed me off. I pushed the men's bathroom door open, walked in, and saw a man standing at the urinal. The first thing I noticed was his dick, and it was big. I didn't even get to look at his face.

"O my God! I'm sorry!" I screamed, closing my eyes, and backed out of the bathroom.

I was so embarrassed. I didn't even think to knock because I was upset. I walked back over to the counter where Lee was, and she had a grin on her face.

"What are you grinning about?"

"You didn't see that fine ass man back there that just came in looking for you. He asked for you by name. You know niggas normally come in here and ask 'where that exotic looking chick at'. There is he is right there."

I turned around and it was the guy from last night. I can't even remember his name. I went behind the counter and ducked down like I was looking at the cigarettes. I knew he wouldn't be able to see me. I was hoping that he would just leave out of the store, but since he came in here looking for me, he probably wouldn't leave until he saw me. My heart was literally beating out of my chest. I mean I wasn't scared of niggas or anything, but I just didn't want to talk to him.

BRANDON

*A*fter Duke hit me up and told me Mickey Mouse's information, I had to go see her. I ain't never had a girl who didn't call me when I gave them my number, so I was a little tight. I put on some basketball shorts, and a black t-shirt with my black Jordan slides. I loved dressing up, but I also loved dressing comfortable too. On the way to the gas station, I picked me up a Route 44 water from Zaxby's, so I could take some medication for the headache that I had. I pulled up to the gas station and went inside. Some chick that I know wasn't Pilar, was at the front.

"Hey, shorty, does a girl by the name of Pilar... Pilar Harrison, work here?"

"Who wants to know?"

"Me. The fuck. Ain't I the one that asked about her?" I asked rudely.

She was starting to get on my nerves. My bladder was full as fuck, so that's probably why I was getting irritated quickly. I'm usually a patient man. Well, for the most part.

"What is your name?" she asked me.

"Does Pilar work here or not? Never mind."

I had to leave that counter before I fucked around and pissed on myself, and that was not going to be a good look. I went in the bathroom and relieved myself. Just as I was finishing, someone burst in the bathroom, and I looked up and it was her. Before I could even say anything, she had apologized and bolted out of the bathroom. It was also a good thing that I knew she was here, because I definitely was not about to go back to that counter and deal with that stupid ass, hating ass bitch that was at the front.

When I walked out of the bathroom, I saw Pilar talking to that girl. When she turned around and looked at me, she went behind the counter and ducked, like I couldn't see her. Yeah, she is probably just as weird as she looks. I picked up some candy so I could add it to my alcohol later tonight, and some beef jerky. I took it to the front and checked out. Shorty told me my total, and the whole time, I'm leaning over the counter looking at Pilar crouching down, like the kids do in school for tornado warnings.

"Um… Ms. Lee." I read her name tag. "Does Ms. Mickey Mouse really think that I can't see her?"

"Okay, Lee, the cigarettes are all stocked," Pilar jumped up and said.

Lee and I both looked at her like she was crazy. We both knew that she wasn't doing anything down there, but hoping I would leave without saying anything to her. She should have known that I wasn't going to leave without saying anything to her, because I came here looking specifically for her.

"Mickey Mouse, when is your break?" I asked her, and she looked at me funny.

"That is not my name, and I don't get a break. The only break I get is when there are no customers in the store."

I looked around and there were no customers in the store.

"I can cover the floor. Go head, Lari," Lee grinned and nudged her.

If her eyes were daggers, then both Lee and I would have been cut the fuck up. She stepped around the corner, and had the tightest smile on her face. We went next door to the chicken place and took a seat. We just sat there staring at each other for a minute.

"So, what's up with you, Ms. Mickey Mouse?" I asked.

"Nothing, but you have to forgive me, I don't remember your name. Please don't call me that. It's straight aggy."

"Oh yeah? Well, what did you do with the card that I gave you? My name and number was on that card."

"Ummm, I kinda threw it away," she said like she didn't just disrespect me by telling me she threw my shit away.

"You *kinda* threw it away… why?" I questioned and eyed her.

"You look like trouble… the type of trouble that I don't need in my life. You were flirting with every girl in Duke's last night. So, I'll pass," she said and rolled her eyes.

"How do I look like trouble?"

"You just do. You probably a thug, have multiple girls, and shit that I don't have time for."

"I can assure you that I'm not a thug. I make my money the legal way." *Most of it… well, half of it,* I thought. "I have girls that are friends, and girls that I fuck, but if I find a girl that is for me, then I will settle down. I see the way you looking at me. I'm not that guy. I don't play with girls' feelings or their hearts. I let them know what it is up front," I lied while smiling.

She rolled her eyes all the way to the ceiling. I could tell that she was going to be a hard fish to catch. I won't stop until I catch it though.

"First of all, you sound ignorant as hell. Why the fuck would you just keep a bundle of bitches until you find one that makes you want to cut them all off? Be the person that you want to find… um, don't be a nickel out here looking for a dime."

"Nah, you just ain't about to hit me with some Lyfe Jennings lyrics. I know the song."

She laughed, and she had the sexiest laugh that I've ever heard. Her voice was even sexy to me. It's not too squeaky and it's not deep. It's like a perfect alto voice. A voice that I would love to hear moaning sweet nothings in my ear.

"I'm laughing, but I'm dead ass. I can't be out in these streets saying that I want a wholesome ass nigga, but I'm just going to be a hoe in the meantime. Yeah… no, it doesn't work that way, my nigga. You need to get your life together or that one girl will never enter your life. You'll die old and lonely with that mindset."

"Damn, you really just got me all the way together, huh? I'll cut off all my hoes for you, right now, if you say yes to me taking you out tonight when you get off."

"I'll be tired. Maybe another day. So, you get to keep your hoes just a little longer."

This girl was literally a class act. I couldn't help but to laugh at her. She was so fucking serious when she said it, which made it even funnier.

"How you know what you gon' feel like when you get off from work?"

"I'm always tired when I get off from work. Tonight won't be any different."

"Well, can you swing by the pool hall tonight for a few minutes? I just want to see you again, Pilar."

"Okay, which bus goes by the pool hall?"

"The bus? You take the bus by yourself when you leave here? What time do you get off?"

I mean, this girl worked in a bad part of Duval County, and I already know how this gas station can jump, especially on the weekends. This particular gas station was always getting robbed. I ain't shit, but I wouldn't let nobody I know catch the bus from this side of town. Damn.

"Dear Lord, you ask so many questions and at the same time, you make it seem like you actually care, but I get off at eleven tonight. The last bus runs over here at like between eleven- eighteen, and eleven-thirty. Every other night when I get off, there is this homeless man by the name of Charlie, who walks me to the bus stop and waits for me to get on the bus, and then he goes back to wherever he goes. He is such a nice man, so I try to buy him dinner every time I can."

"Wait, wait, wait, let me make sure I get this straight. Pilar, you let a homeless man walk you to the bus stop when you get off? He has never tried anything with you?"

"Oh my god! You act like I said an extraterrestrial person walks me to the bus stop. Charlie is a very nice man, and he has been nothing but a gentleman to me since I met him almost a year ago. So, there's that. Some nights, Swan can't make it to pick me up, so he makes sure no one bothers me. I mean, if you noticed, this is not the best part of Jacksonville."

"Pilar, I'm coming to pick you up tonight. End of discussion."

I held my hand up before she could protest because I know her little feisty ass was not trying to ride with me. Every time she tried to say something, I held my hand up, so she finally just gave in.

"Fine. Don't be late either, or me and Charlie will be heading to the fucking bus stop," she snapped.

She got up and walked away. While she was walking away, my eyes were glued to her little petite ass. She was what they call slim thick. She was little, but that body was snatched. I can't wait to get a full view of that ass bouncing on my dick. I licked my lips at the thought of it. I grabbed my keys and headed home.

∞

"Come on, come on, come on," I mumbled to myself as I sat at the slot machine pulling on the lever.

See, I wasn't supposed to come here. I was on my way home, but I saw the billboard for the casino, and I swear my car just kept driving on its own. I was doing fine and hadn't gambled since I almost lost my life a couple of months ago. A couple of months ago, I was sitting at the poker table, gambling my bill money away, but I wasn't worried because I was just going to have one of my hoes to pay it. I pulled one of my cards that I kept under the table, waited until it was my turn, and put the card on the table. I had won damn near two thousand dollars. I took my earnings, but when I stood up, the other card fell from my lap. I thought that I had put back in the tiny slot. I tried to bolt out the door, but those old men were fast as shit. They beat my ass within an inch of my life, and I told myself that I would never gamble again, but here I am. I hadn't been back to that casino since then. It was a good thing that Duke didn't know about this problem that I had, or he wouldn't have hired me to be his general manager.

I honestly don't know if gambling is hereditary or not, but I used to watch my mom and grandma gamble all our money away, until they had to end up sucking dick or selling shit in the house to get the damn bills paid. I mean aside from the fact that it's addictive, it is stress relieving; well, if you are winning.

"Shit, I almost had it. I'm only going to play one more time. That is going to be it," I whispered to myself.

Who am I kidding? I said that twenty times ago, and I'm still sitting here. It's like the lights and the sounds had me hypnotized. As soon as I spun the lever, I felt a hand on my shoulder and I almost fell out the seat.

"Blizzy, my man. How are you?"

I turned around and it was on of Duke's brothers, Baron. The one that was next to him in age.

"What's up, Baron? You scared me. What are you doing here?"

I thought I was getting away from everybody when I came to a different casino thirty miles from Jacksonville. I didn't want to see anybody I knew.

"Well, I'm just trying to see what we could add to Duke's to make it better, and I came here to get ideas."

"Yeah, that's what I was doing too. I just sat down a few minutes ago, and started seeing if I could win over here."

"Ah, okay. It's getting close to time for Duke's to open, are you going tonight?"

"What you mean, it's getting close to time for Duke's to open... it's only—"

"Eleven," Baron finished my sentence.

Oh Shit! Pilar! I thought to myself.

"I have to go, B. Good seeing you."

I grabbed my things and bolted out the door. I jumped in my car and sped away. I never did get her number so I couldn't call her. I googled the number to the gas station, called, but there was no answer. Man, I swear I sat down at the slot machine at like seven, so how the hell did four hours go by that damn fast. It don't even seem like I was sitting there that fucking long. Man, what the fuck is wrong with me? If I could change anything in the world, I swear it would be this fucking gambling addiction. I sped like a bat out of hell towards Pilar's job. I'm glad I had the sports edition of the BMW, because this mothafucka could get on down.

I made it to the gas station in record time. I slowly crept through the parking lot of the gas station, and I didn't see her inside. I pulled slowly around the corner to head to the bus stop, and that's when I saw

Pilar in an orange safety vest, along with a man who I assumed was Charlie. I pulled alongside them and stopped the car.

PILAR

*W*hen it was close to time to get off, Swan had text me and asked me if I needed a ride, and I had told her that I was good on the ride. I was low-key hyping myself up over this ride that I was getting from whatever his name was. He never told me what his name was again. I can admit that he was a little a cutie, but I'm sure that along with being cute, he had baggage and shit.

"So, you're actually going to get in the car with that guy?" Lee asked me as I was stocking the Cigarellos. They come and go so fast, especially on the weekends.

"Yeah, I am. He literally gave me no choice. I told him if he is not here at eleven, then I will be on my way to the bus stop. I think he's harmless. If I don't show up to work tomorrow, then you have his face on camera," I said as I laughed.

"Girl, that ain't nothing to be laughing at. You know niggas these days are crazy, especially niggas from Duval."

"Girl, I ain't worried about a nigga from Duval no more than I am worried about a nigga from Mount Olive, Mississippi, and I swear every nigga I know from Mississippi is crazy… like legit ass crazy. If I can protect myself from them, then I can protect myself from a Duval ass nigga. I keep mace and a blade with me."

I clocked out right at eleven, and when I walked outside, there was no one waiting, at least not for me. I sat on the bench outside the gas station, waited for a couple of minutes and there was nothing. I should have known not to trust that this nigga would be here on time. I ain't trusted a nigga since the first nigga broke my heart, and that was Prince Harrison. Back home, I only used these niggas for what they were good for: dick. I'm sure that I probably missed out on a lot of good dudes in college because of that mentality, but the first time they did something that made me question whether I trusted them or not, I got ghost. So, I ain't never had my heart broke by a boyfriend, and I don't ever plan on it.

"Ms. Pilar, how are you doing tonight. How was work?" Charlie asked, walking up to me.

The first time he approached me, I wasn't too scared because like I said, I kept my mace and my blade on me. He offered to walk me to the bus stop, and that started our relationship. He has always been very nice and respectful of me. I buy him dinner when I can, but he has never, not one time, asked me for any money.

"Hey, Charlie. Work was fine. I was sitting out here waiting for someone who said they were going to pick me up, but I guess we can head to the bus stop now. What you been doing all day?"

He handed me his safety vest that he wears when he is walking the streets late at night.

"You know me. I been doing what I always do. So, who was supposed to come pick you up?"

"So, I met this guy last night. I can't think of his name right now. He came into the station earlier today, and told me that he was going to pick me up today. All niggas be lying. I have come to that conclusion."

"Well, Ms. Pilar, I don't think all niggas lie. He may have gotten held up or something. Has he called or text you?"

"Well, he doesn't have my number. He gave me his number last night at the pool hall, but I threw the number away. He may have an agenda, what you think?"

"Well, I don't think that you should get in the car with a man and you don't even know his name; however, I think that you should give someone a chance to get in that cold heart of yours, Ms. Pilar. You don't have to be so mean all the time. All men are not the same."

"I know all men are not the same, duh. Every man is different, but the game don't change."

"Touché, Ms. Pilar, touché," he laughed.

Charlie and I talked a lot about me, but never about him. All I knew really was his name, and that he was homeless. He looked like he could be just a few years older than me. Before I could say anything else, the prettiest and shiniest Beamer pulled up and just sat there.

"Is that your friend, Ms. Pilar?"

"I don't know," I whispered to him.

The door opened and he stepped out. It looks like he was much taller than he was earlier when I first saw him. Him and Charlie stood about neck and neck.

"Mick... Pilar, I'm so sorry. Time got away from me. I still want to give you a ride," he said.

"What is your name?" Charlie asked him.

"Why?" he spat.

"I'm not letting her get in the car with a man and she doesn't even know his name," Charlie said stepping in front of me.

I love being protected. Charlie gives me such a big brother vibe.

"Blizzy."

"Blizzy," Charlie and I said in unison, and started laughing.

"Pilar, are you coming, 'cause I kinda have to get to work?" he asked me.

"Charlie, I will see you tomorrow. Here is ten bucks. Go get you something to eat on," I said smiling at him. I handed him his vest back.

"Ms. Pilar, I told you about giving me money. I'm fine. You need the money more than I do, trust me."

"Are you sure?" I questioned.

"Yes… yes, I'm sure. Here, you can reach me on this number if you need me," he said, and he put a number in my phone.

I gave him a hug and got in the car with Blizzy. As soon as I got in the car, Blizzy went into attack mode with the questions.

"Are you sure that nigga homeless? He don't look homeless to me. How the fuck he got a phone? Where do you know him from?"

I instantly put my fingers in my ear because he always asking so many questions. It's so annoying. He snatched one of my hands out of my ear.

"You real childish, you know that?"

"Nah, you *real* childish, for being an adult and letting people— grown people, call you Blizzy. What the hell is your real name?"

"Brandon, now answer all my questions about that nigga... Charles."

"It's Charlie, and I don't know much about him. He doesn't talk about himself. All I know is his name and he's homeless."

"Mickey Mouse, you so naïve. I been living here all my life, and I have been coming to this gas station all my life, and I ain't never seen that nigga a day in my life. All of a sudden, he just popped up and started walking you to the bus stop every other night out of the *goodness* of his *heart*."

"Look, just because you expect something from every bitch you do something nice for, that don't mean he is the same way. If we are going to talk about Charlie the whole way, then you can drop me off right here."

"Aight, my bad, man. We finna go to the pool hall. I have to check on shit there."

"Cool," I said and let the seat back.

"So, tell me about Ms. Mickey Mouse. What do I need to know about her before I become her man?"

"Um, it's funny, because I never really talk about myself. What do you want to know, ask me questions?"

"I did just ask you a question, but I guess I can be more specific. Where are you from? Tell me a little about your life."

"I am from a small town in Mississippi called Mount Olive. It's very, very small, and everybody knows everybody. Ummm, I graduated at the top of my class in high school, and I went to college at Jackson State University and got a degree in Health Science. I was born a crackhead..." He swerved into another lane almost causing a wreck.

"My bad. You caught me way off guard."

"Anyways, I was a born a crackhead. My mother was a crackhead, and was turned out by my raggedy ass pappy, Prince Harrison. That's what I believe, and no one will be able to tell me different. In my younger years, I cooked and cut crack, and measured cocaine. Yes, I still know how, but don't fucking ask me too ever. Some shit you just don't forget. She overdosed on my very first day of high school. I didn't even cry because I was happy she was no longer on Earth fighting that demon. My grandmother, Lenora, tried to do her best to care for me before I found her dead. I'm sure she smoked and drank herself to death."

"Jesus fucking Christ, Pilar. Let's go back to a happy place in your life, 'cause got damn. I don't even know what to ask you anymore; you just fucked my mind all the way up."

"It's fine, I think I turned out just fine. I don't do drugs. Well, I get high and drink a little, but I don't do that often. I like museums, slow walks on the beach, and art. I like random shit, like nobody else like... like clouds and shit. I can't wait until I'm able to travel the world. If that lightens the mood a little. So, tell me about you."

Brandon told me about his high school career playing sports, and his college career playing football. It made me a little sad that he had his football career snatched away from him by a hating ass nigga, and at least he was in jail for the rest of his life for the bullshit. He didn't talk much about his family though, and I don't blame him, especially if his family was anything like mine. We pulled up to Duke's and he opened the door for me.

"How long are we going to be here?"

"Just for a little while. I have to show my face around here, sometimes. I mean, since I am the general manager."

"Well, excuse the hell out of me, *general manager*. I'll make myself comfortable until you finish doing what you do," I said, and he gave me smirk while biting his bottom lip.

This nigga was going to be trouble. I mean, I'm not going to even pretend like I didn't see that big dick earlier in the bathroom, and the even bigger print in those basketball shorts that he had on. Twenty minutes later, I saw Brandon again and he was freshly dressed in a tailored suit, looking good as hell. He was just making his way around the crowd, talking to people, and giving out his cards, like he was doing last night when I first met him. My phone started ringing and I looked down and it was Swan.

"Hello," I answered the phone.

It had only been two minutes and Brandon was no longer in my sight. I started walking around so I could put my eyes on him again.

"Bitch, where the fuck you at? I'm damn near headed to the police station to file a missing person's report on your ass, and what the fuck is all that noise?"

"Swan, calm down. I am at the place where we came last night, with the guy from last night."

"Bitch, what the fuck you mean you with the guy from last night? How did you get with him? You threw his number away. Are you safe?"

"Look, I will have to explain it to you later, and yes, I'm safe."

"Alright, bitch. I'm about to send you a video. I'm glad you safe, though. I'll see you later," she hurriedly said and hung up.

Not even a whole minute later, my damn phone went off with a text message from Swan.

Swan: 1 video attached. *Pilar, I was swear to God I'm in love.*

I opened the video, and it was a video of Swan getting fucked by the white neighbor. She was moaning his name and he was moaning hers. He was legit fucking the shit out of her. His dick definitely put the color-to-big dick ratio to shame. The man had length and girth like a mothafucka. I couldn't even tear my eyes away from the fucking video. Yeah, this is the type of friends that me and Swan were. We sent each other videos of our sexcapades. We didn't particularly have a reason for doing it, but we did. I was still watching the video, and the neighbor, Bryan, had just asked Swan if she wanted to be his mistress, when I heard someone clear their throat.

"Excuse me," a very deep voice said, along with an accent.

"You're excused," I said, not even looking up.

"I was trying to be nice, but you're in my way," he retorted with an attitude.

"Why don't you just…" I lost my words when I looked up into the most handsome chocolate face I had ever seen. This man was a dark god. I looked him up and down, and he did the same thing to me. We could barely pull our eyes away from each other. I looked around, and it was more than enough space for him to walk around me.

"Why don't I just what? This my mothafuckin' place, and everybody knows when they see me they get the fuck out the way," he snapped.

"Well, first of all, apparently, everybody don't know who the fuck you are, because here I am. You can walk your ass around. Who the fuck do you think you are?" I snapped right back.

"Bitch, let me—"

"I got your mothafuckin'—"

"Pilar, baby, I was looking for you. I see that you met my boss, Duke Ramses," Brandon said from behind me.

"You have one rude mothafuckin' boss," I said to him. "I don't see how he's somebody's boss. I couldn't dare work for him."

"Well it's good that you don't then. I've said way too much to you. You need to leave before I break your fucking neck," he said with a glare that would have scared me if I hadn't been through everything that I have been through.

We just stared at each other before Brandon pulled me away from him.

"I'll get out of this piece of shit," I said and shot him the bird.

Brandon and I walked to his car and got in. He told me to put my address in his GPS system and we rode in silence for the first fifteen minutes.

"Out of all the people you could have gotten into it with tonight, you choose to get into it with my boss," Brandon finally spoke.

"You have a rude ass boss, and I don't know where the fuck he from, but that shit don't fly over here. That nigga in America." I laughed.

"Anyways, are you going to always be this problematic everywhere I take you?"

"He started with me, what the fuck? I was minding my own got damn business, and he approached me talking shit, like he King Tut or some-fucking-body. He better be glad you intervened or it probably would have gotten uglier than it already was. I don't care that he's damn near two feet taller than me. The bigger they are, the harder they fall."

Brandon laughed at me, and I'm sure that he probably thought I was crazy. I am, but I'm real as fuck. If Lenora didn't teach me anything else, she always taught me to stand up for myself, and to never let nobody run over me. He turned on some old-school jams. Songs like that always get me in the mood. I looked over at him, and he was bobbing his head along to Rome's, "I Belong To You". He was also biting his bottom lip, and that shit was so fucking sexy to me.

Twenty minutes later, we pulled up in front of my place.

"Pilar, can I be honest with you about something?"

"Why wouldn't you be?"

"I want to eat your pussy. Like, I all of a sudden just got the urge to want to eat your pussy. That's all I been thinking about on this ride home. I want to rip your pants off right now and eat your pussy. I bet it's pretty and shit. You're so fucking exotic that you probably got it pierced and shit. Pilar, I want to make love to your pussy and ass with my mouth… right… now."

I wasn't necessarily taken aback by his honesty because that is something that I get all the time, especially working at that gas station. I have heard worse.

"Since we are being honest, I really don't like oral sex. Well, I don't like receiving, I like to give. I know what you are thinking… somebody not eating my pussy right. Trust me, I have had some good pussy eaters, it just doesn't do anything for me…unless it's a woman. I'm not saying that men can't give good head, but it's like women know how to please other women."

He just stared at me like I had two heads on my shoulders. I love sex… everything about it, except someone eating my pussy. Well, unless a female is eating my pussy. I'm bisexual, but me fucking a bitch comes few and far between. I love sucking dick though. The fact that I can suck a man's soul out of his body, gives me so much life. I like having control over men.

"So, you like to suck dick?" he asked me as he started unzipping his slacks.

"Yes," I whispered.

"You want to suck this one?" he asked me as he started to stroke his dick.

I had a good view of it because of the streetlight that we were parked directly under. It was long, thick, yellow, with a pink head… the exact same color of his lips. He let the seat back, and guided my head over to his dick.

"Record me." I handed him my phone, and he turned on the camera.

I started kissing on the head of his dick and kissed all the way down his shaft until I reached the bottom of it. I came back up and started licking the pre-cum that was oozing from his dick. I put the head of his dick in my warm mouth and sucked lightly, and then went down inch by inch, holding it tightly in my mouth, and then came back up. I made sure to wet his dick all the way up before I started using my hands. I grabbed his dick with both hands and started stroking him while sucking at the same time.

"Sssssssss, Pilar," he whispered. "This shit feels so fucking amazing. Keep doing it like that, baby."

Nothing I loved more than a little motivation during head. He used his free hand to start rubbing his hands through my thick ass curly hair.

"Damn, baby, this your real fucking hair? Damnnnnnn, don't fucking stop, P," he groaned.

I started going faster, but now my hands were going in different directions, while going up and down on his dick. I could feel my juices flowing out of my pussy. Look, sucking dick turns me all the way on.

"Shit, baby, you sucking like you want something to come out of this mothafucka."

I kept going, and I felt his dick starting to pulsate in my mouth. He was getting ready to nut. I stuck one of my hands in his pants and started massaging his balls. He grabbed my head and started guiding me up and down his dick faster and faster. I didn't care because my gag reflex was on point. He shoved my head down on his dick, and shot his warm ass nut down my throat. I felt him starting to go soft in my mouth, and I started back bobbing my head up and down on his dick.

"Oh my fucking god, Pilar. Shit! Baby! Shit! Ooowweee, come on, lil' mama… fuck!"

He kept trying to pull me off his dick, but he couldn't, and he just let me do my thing until I was finished. I came up, licking my lips, and wiped my mouth on the sleeve of my shirt. He was just staring at me, and it was starting to get awkward.

"I think I messed up your seats. I'm sorry." I apologized because I could feel that my juices were soaking through my pants and into his cloth seats. I had on a thong so that was part of the problem.

"Let me feel it." He reached over and put his hands between my legs and felt the wetness. His eyes got big as saucers. He unbuttoned my pants, and stuck his hand in them, and started playing with my pussy through my thong.

"Pilar, you really got this wet from sucking my dick? Let me taste this shit."

"Nah, I have gas station pussy and ass right now. I have to go shower," I protested.

"What the fuck did I just say? Get the fuck out them pants," he ordered.

I did exactly what he said. I don't know how he was going to eat my pussy because he was so fucking tall. He leaned my seat back as far as it would go, and told me to get on all fours. Once I did that, he started eating my pussy from the back. This man moved his tongue so fast over my clit, and I was going crazy trying to get away from him. He wrapped his one arm around my waist and I was stuck as shit, so I just started twerking on his tongue as he ate my pussy. I guess he liked that because he started smacking my ass and moaning into my pussy. He stuck two fingers in me, and I instantly clinched my pussy muscles on his fingers. He pulled back, and leaned back in his seat, and started stroking his dick.

"Aye, I got to have you. Come sit your ass on this dick."

He went into his console and pulled out a rubber, and slid it on his dick. I crawled over the armrest, and positioned myself facing the steering wheel.

"You want me to record this too?"

I nodded my head, as I slid on his thick ass dick. I closed my eyes at the feeling of him making himself comfortable inside of my walls.

"Shhhhiiiittt, baby... You fucking me up. This the best shit I ever slid in," he moaned as I started bouncing on his dick, making sure to twerk my ass.

"You like that, daddy?"

"Hell yeahhhh, keep making this ass clap." He kept smacking my ass.

"Oooowweee, baby, daddy wants you to cum with him, 'cause I'm getting ready to fucking explode."

"I'm finna cummm, baby," I moaned out.

I did this little shake shit that I do with my legs, when I'm pretending to cum. Yeah, that's right, a bitch that loves sex doesn't even cum during sex. I got a broken pussy. I can make myself cum when I play with my vibrator, but with male stimulation, no.

"Oooweee, baby, I feel it," he moaned out.

I rolled my eyes at the lie, but I kept going up and down on his dick until he exploded in the condom. I sat on him and contracted my walls on his dick. He loved that shit, and started getting back on hard, but I got up, and got back over on the passenger side.

"Shit, he was waking back up. Why you get up?"

"I'm not the general manager of a store and can go in as I please. I have to get inside and get to bed. I had a really nice time with you, Brandon," I said while grabbing my things, getting out of the car.

"Damn, can I at least walk you to the damn door? I mean, I don't want you to feel like that's the only thing that I wanted from you. Can I get a hug or a kiss or something?" he questioned.

I have had so many one-night stands that I didn't even think about it. I let him walk me to the door. I gave him a hug and dodged his kiss. I know it was weird that I just fucked this nigga and won't kiss him, but kissing is… just something that I don't do. I have kissed before, but I just didn't like it. It didn't feel right, so I just stopped doing it. I know most people would look at me like I'm a hoe for fucking a nigga on the first night, but I'm grown and I don't do anything that I'm ashamed of. He was consenting and so was I, so there's that. Some of the best sex you probably will ever have, comes from a one-night stand. I walked into the dark house and felt my way to my room. I smiled at the thought of Brandon's good ass dick. I could only imagine what that nigga would do to me in a fucking bed. I had just pulled my clothes off when I received a text message.

904-555-8891: *Goodnight, beautiful. Tonight was fucking* *wonderful. I just want you to know that I ain't tryna make this no one time thing. I legit wanna date the fuck out of you. Lol! That sex will just be a fucking bonus. Lock me in. -Blizzy*

I smiled at the text message. I was too tired to even take a shower, so I just dove in the fucking bed. As soon as my head hit the pillow, I was out like a light.

DUKE

$\mathcal{M}$y brothers and I followed Baron with our eyes as he paced the living room floor.

"Duke, are you listening to me?" Baron questioned. "Some' ain't right about that nigga."

I was irritated as shit because I was in the middle of a massage, when Baron, Bomani, and Bakari barged into my house, unannounced, and definitely uninvited. I know we all live in close proximity, but they still call before they come their asses over. I definitely have to remind these niggas that their keys are used for emergencies only.

"I guess I really don't have a choice but to listen, now do I?" I replied, while rubbing my temples with a blunt in my hand.

I guess this had to be important, because my brothers know that I am a by the schedule type of guy, and if I have to deviate from that then I really get irritated. Like right now, it's 11:19 in the morning and I'm supposed to be moaning to the soft touch of those Asian chicks' hands on my back, not listening to my fucking brother talk about some shit that I don't care to listen to.

"Duke, you can get back to your fucking massage in a minute. Just hear him out," Bakari spat.

I cut my eyes at him and he matched my evil stare. This nigga really been trying to get buck within the last couple of months since he had gained about fifty pounds of muscle. He must not know that I will still drop his ass on his fucking head with no hesitation. His little ass must be due for a reminder or something. I'll get back to his ass in a minute.

"You have the floor, Baron."

"Okay, so check this out. You know that casino I been going to outside of Jax, getting ideas to make our shit better?"

He looked at me like he wanted me to answer the question. I just shrugged so he could continue.

"Well, I seen him there the first time about two months ago, and he was just chilling. Two hours later, he was still sitting in the same spot. I walked up to him and pretended like I had just walked in, and he was looking strung out. When I mentioned to him about getting to work, he bolted out of the casino like he had a complete lapse of time. So—"

"Baron, I swear to God, I love you. I love you with all my heart, but I really need you to headline this story for me."

"I believe your general manager has a gambling problem and has been stealing from Duke's, and also from the customers. I just can't put my finger on it just yet. I know—"

"Wait, wait, wait… just wait one damn minute," I roared. "You three barged into my massage session, interrupting me, because of a *hunch*. Get out. It's 11:30, and they're supposed to be working on my neck by now," I said, looking at the face of my diamond Rolex.

"That's your fucking problem, you don't never listen to nobody. You think you know every fucking thing and you don't. I hope that nigga robs you fucking blind," Bakari said, standing over me.

I looked up at him and he was seething. I don't know where all this anger came from, but he needed to get that shit in check.

"Bakari, you of all people know I don't like niggas standing over me. I don't know where this surge of confidence came from, but you need to move out the way. Let me get back to the massage that's supposed to be on my neck right now before I drop you on yours."

"Fuck you!" he spat and then tried to hit me with a right hook, but I blocked it and had him hemmed up against the wall before he could even swing his left arm.

"Kari, what the fuck is wrong with you? That's our big brother," Bomani yelled.

"He don't never listen to nobody, and he think…shit, let me go, Duke, you hurting me."

"Don't you think you would have hurt me if you would have connected with that right hook? Bakari, I don't know what's gotten into you, but if you want to talk like men then you need to hit me up personally, and not on this weak shit you trying to do. Boy, I can kill you. Chill out," I spat and then threw him to the floor.

I reached down to help him up and he grabbed my hand to get up. I guess he needed a reminder that I can still beat his little ass. I love all my brothers to death but if I have to put one on their ass, then I swear I won't hesitate.

"Baron, I am in no way trying to downplay your information, but you know I only work with facts and not no hunches. Bring me some more concrete information and then we will act on it. Aight?"

"Yeah, big bro. Sorry for interrupting your massage. I'mma get you your evidence," Baron said, and they all filed out of my house so I could go back to my massage.

Baron has got to be reaching, or is he? I mean, I have found him a few times more than normal, sitting at a slot machine when he was supposed to be working. I mean, who wouldn't get distracted by all those lights in the room. I mean, sometimes I find myself playing them too, and it's my own damn place. I hope that is the reason, because if I find out that he has in fact been doing all this shit Baron been saying he's been doing, I'mma murk that nigga. I'm about my business but if you come between that, I will not hesitate to do what I have to do. I've done it before.

After my massage, I decided to head over to the pool hall. During the day, it's basically a lounge spot where you can just chill, watch TV, and work. Free wi-fi attracts most of the college kids. You can also host book club meetings, baby showers, and all types of events because I have an event room at the back of the building. When I walked in, it was packed. I saw a bunch of the college students sitting spread out in the chairs and laid out of the floor, appearing to be working. My lounge caters to everybody. It's basically like a glorified Starbucks. I ain't no fool now, you have to have your ID to get in, and you get a wristband that correlates to your age. I ain't trying to go to jail because a little chump wants to get on the slot machines, and they're not twenty-one. The gambling side is open during the day, but only a few machines that are closer to the front so they can be monitored. As soon as ten o'clock hits, the young ones have to leave and it's straight twenty-one and up. I loved this place.

I was kicked back in my office watching the cameras, when Pilar and Blizzy came through the door. For the last couple of months, they had been kicking it tough. I honestly think Blizzy has fallen in love with her, and her young ass is probably just playing him. She doesn't seem to be as into him as he is into her. I watched the cameras, and it looked like they were on their way to my office. I put my feet down and powered down the monitor when I heard the knock on my door.

"It's open," I yelled.

They came in, and my eyes were instantly on Pilar. She is a pistol, and she would have been dead if she lived in Egypt. She had on this form fitting dress, hugging that petite ass body. I roamed her body like I always do, and then focused my attention back on Brandon, who was standing there looking at me funny. I guess he realized I was eye fucking Pilar's weird looking ass. As much as I hated her, I would fuck that bad ass attitude right the fuck out of her. I'm going to fuck her, but I just don't know when.

"What's up, Blizzy?" I nodded at him. "Bitch," I acknowledged Pilar.

I know that got under her skin, because her little face started to turn beet red, and that gave me much satisfaction since I can't kill her. Brandon knows not to say anything when I speak to Pilar because I will bust his ass with the mothafuckin' quickness.

"Fuck boy," she spat back at me, rolling her eyes and neck

simultaneously. "You gon' stop fucking with me, you rude ass bitch. If you can't say 'hey Pilar' or even just a simple 'hey', then don't fucking speak at all. It's all so simple."

My left eye started twitching, because I wanted to kill her, and I wanted to fuck her. Dear God, this little bitch was giving me so many mixed emotions and I couldn't control it. Since that first encounter we had, I wanted to bend her ass over the table and fuck her senseless. Blizzy can't be hitting that right because she is so fucking mouthy. I ain't never met a woman this fucking mouthy. Her dad couldn't have been around her. If I was fucking her, she would know to shut the fuck up when two men are in the room talking.

"Okay, guys! Now that the pleasantries are over, Duke, I was coming to tell you that I need to be off this weekend. I need to go out of town with Pilar."

I looked at Pilar, who was staring at her phone, and then back at him.

"No. I need you this weekend."

"Duke—"

"No, I *need* you this weekend," I said with more finality.

"Brandon, I told you this was a waste of time. You should have never come here to begin with. It's okay, I can go by myself. He is only doing this to spite me, with his ugly ass," she spat to him while looking at me.

Her face was turning red again and she walked closer to my desk, slamming her hand on my desk, thinking she was startling me. I laughed, thinking that I could eat that little fist for an afternoon snack.

"Look, stupid ass, I don't like you, and you don't like me. That's clear, but Brandon has been working his ass off ever since this janky ass place opened… non-stop. You can give him the weekend off. You ain't doing shit but being a bitch ass nigga that needs to get knocked off his high horse. You put your panties on the same way I do, one leg at a fucking time."

I laughed so hard inside. This little girl really think she's something, banging on my desk and getting in my face. I raised up and got even closer to her face. My nose was damn near on her nose. My dick started to get hard. Fuck! I hate this broad.

"I eat little bitches like you for dinner, literally. Don't you question me and the decisions that I make regarding my business. If I said no then the answer is fucking no, and that's fucking final. You can't scare me into making a decision, bitch," I hissed through gritted teeth.

"You ain't got to be scared to get your big ass sliced and diced. You must don't know the bigger they are, the harder they fucking fall," she hissed back, and then moved her tongue in her cheek, putting the blade between her teeth, and then moving it back, like it never happened.

Her face was red and her chest was heaving up and down like she was a bull. I could smell her minty fresh breath, and I wanted to take her tongue in my mouth and suck so lightly on it.

"Pilar, let's go," Brandon said from behind us, but we both kept a deathly glare on each other.

"Yeah, Blizz, that'll be best, before this bitch be floating under the Matthews Bridge," I spat, while continuously getting lost in her green eyes and full pouty ass lips. I was so lost in her eyes that I missed her hand raise.

SMACK!

Her small ass hand came across my face, making my face turn just a little. I closed my eyes because my face was stinging. Damn! This little bitch.

"You listen to me. You can call me anything you want to call me, but you better not ever in your black stupid life threaten my life, or we will be both floating under the Matthews Bridge," she spat in my face. "Now I'm ready to go, Brandon." She rolled her eyes at me, then stomped away, pulling Brandon with her. He mouthed 'sorry' to me, and they walked out the door.

I sat back in my seat and started grinning to myself, because that little girl just don't know she is in a world of trouble. I could have let Brandon off this weekend, but I was going home. Well, I didn't need him, and I could have just used one of my brothers, but I wanted to keep him away from Pilar as much as I could. I ain't no hating ass nigga or nothing, but I know the more he was here, the more that I could see Pilar and get under her skin.

∞

When my jet landed in Egypt, I couldn't have been happier. I get to see my fiancée, my father, and my mothers. As soon as I stepped off the plane, the sun kissed me smack in the face. It was hotter than a bitch out here. I walked through the people that were bowing for me. Here, I wasn't Duke. Here, I am Barak the Prince, son of Barak the King. I can do whatever I want to do over here, with no repercussions.

I took advantage of that shit when I was younger. I jumped in the Rolls Royce that was waiting for me, and headed towards the palace. My brothers normally come with me, but they had their own thing going on and I didn't want to bother them.

"The Prince is here, the Prince is here!" I heard, and looked out my window and saw some little kids running next to the car. They were probably about ten or eleven years old.

I let down the window and told the driver to stop the car. I loved kids, and I never want them to think that I didn't have time for them.

"What's going on, y'all?"

"How long are you going to be here? You still owe me a game of basketball."

"What's your name? I'll invite you and your friends personally to my house to play a game of ball. You can come tomorrow afternoon."

"My name is Chyro."

"Alright, Chyro. I'm locking your name in my phone. Bring your friends tomorrow and we can play. How about that?"

"I can come to your house house? Like, where the King sleeps?" he beamed excitedly.

"Yes, now I won't guarantee that the King will be there; but yes, where the King sleeps."

"Oh my God! Cool. Cool."

I let the window up, and continued on to my dad's house. I put on my prince attire which consisted of a pure ivory silk button up shirt and bottoms. They almost kind of look like pajamas, but they are not.

My dad wears pure white silk. Twenty minutes later, we eased through the gates of the palace.

"Sonnn, you're home," my mom, Isis, said in her deep Arabic accent, and kissed me on my forehead.

My other moms, Nubia, who is Baron's mom; Calandra, Bakari's mom; and Gamila, Bomani's mom, came around the corner, and kissed me on the forehead as well. They were all happy to see me. I don't ever see anything like this working in the United States. Those women over there are crazy as hell and probably would kill each other before they all lived comfortable like this.

"Where is Edwina?" I asked no one in particular.

"She's in her room sleeping," Isis said, and they were all smiling at me.

I raised my eyebrows at them. I made my way towards Edwina's room but I heard footsteps behind me. I turned around and my mothers stopped in their footsteps and were grinning.

"What is going on? Why are y'all following me?" I laughed at them.

They all shook their heads and turned around and walked away. I opened the door to the Edwina's room and there she was sleeping, peacefully. I pulled the covers back and she had on a sexy two-piece lingerie set. Over the years, her body hadn't changed much. She kept herself in shape because it was a requirement from me. She still hadn't stirred as I got between her legs and started kissing on her moist middle. She had to have been having a wet dream. I slid my very long tongue down the center of her pussy lips.

"Mmmmmm, Ba… Prince. I missed you," she whispered holding my head in her center.

I kissed up her mound, around her navel, and then around her stomach, and then I all of sudden stopped.

"Edwina? What the fuck is going on?"

"Huh?" she moaned sleepily.

"Don't fucking 'huh' me. What the fuck is going on? Your fucking stomach wasn't like this last time I came here."

"I wanted to wait, baby, but we are having a baby. The doctor confirmed that I was two months pregnant today." She smiled at me. "Exactly eight weeks."

The wheels started turning in my head, but nah, Edwina loved me and I loved her. She would never cheat on me, at least I hope not.

"How did this happen?" I asked, scratching my head.

"Seriously, Prince?"

"Yes… well, no… yes, I don't know. I just thought we were being careful," I sighed.

We both were quiet and deep in our own thoughts. I wasn't too mad and I wasn't too happy. It's just the fact that I wanted to become a father after I was married and settled in being the King. How am I going to make time to be a father, be the King, and be going back and forth between here and the United States? A baby really changes things for me.

"So, what now?" she asked me, bringing me out of my thoughts.

"I don't know. I'm thinking. I mean, I would never ask you to get rid of it or anything like that. You know that's against the rules. I guess we just have to get ready for a baby."

"Baby, you know you can always move me to the States. I wouldn't mind going over there and seeing what you're living like over there. I would like to visit your businesses and see who… what you've been doing over there."

I was smiling at her, but in my head, that was a no. I was not about to mess up my endless supply of pussy before I got married because she wanted to move over there. I'd been telling her for the last few years that I would take her over there to see all the businesses, but I ain't never made good on that promise.

"I'm going to take you over there. You just have to give me some time," I said, putting a strand of hair behind her ear. "I'm going to let you get some rest. I have to go speak with the King about something. I love you."

I kissed her on her forehead and tucked her back in. I walked around the house to see if I could find my father. If he wasn't in the house, he probably was on the golf course out back. I jumped on a golf cart, and rode around the trail to the golf cart, and there he was.

"Ah, Prince, how long have you been here?"

"I just touched down not too long ago. I went to go get me some sex but I found out that Edwina is pregnant. I talked to you last week… why did you let me walk in on an ambush like that?"

"That's not my place to tell you that, son. Are you ready to be a father? I know you've been living the life of a bachelor over there in the States. You know a kid changes everything," he said, swinging the golf stick.

"Yeah, I know. I honestly wasn't planning on being a father until after I became King. I wanted to be settled back in over here before we brought a kid into this world. I swear, I'm not even sure if—"

"Edwina would never. She doesn't go anywhere unless she is with my wives. She is always in the house preparing to be a good wife for you. If she was cheating on you under my roof, she would have been dead by now. I don't want to hear anything else about that."

When the King finalizes a conversation, you don't say anything else about it, especially if you don't want to be struck with anything in his hand.

"So have you talked to Bakari? That lil' dude been on one. Over the last couple of months, I have been having to put him on his ass and remind him who the fuck the big brother is. I been taking care of him, Bomani, and Baron since I was sixteen years old, and he is the one that gave me the most problems and still does. I don't know what the fuck I did or am doing wrong with him."

"You know them fellas don't talk to me much. Have you tried sitting down with him?"

"Yeah, I have, but he said he's good. I guess he just wants to knock me out one good time, just to say he did it." I laughed.

"You been to see your grandpa?"

"Nah, I'm about to head up there right now."

"Quick question; why aren't you using your security detail? They are over there just chilling and laying around like that's what I pay them to do."

"First of all, no one over there knows my identity and I plan on keeping it that way. I don't want to cause that much attention to myself. It's really no big deal, Father. Everybody over there knows me as Duke Ramses. It ain't like I got to tell them bitches I'm the son of a King to get pussy or some shit." I laughed. "I know a couple of them follow me everywhere I go because of your orders, but as long as they're not making themselves known, then we good."

Even though my dad sent me to the States when I was sixteen, I knew he wanted to keep us safe. I know he had men watching us because I ain't that crazy. They never intervened in my life. They just watched from a distance.

"Alright, son. It looks like you just got life figured all out. I'll let you go see your grandparents. I'm going to hit a few more balls before I come in."

My dad and I hugged and I jumped back on the golf cart and headed back towards the palace. My grandpa is also Barak Ramses, but he is called Dane. He is seventy years old and has a lot of wisdom. He still gets around like he is in his early fifties. My grandmother is the beautiful Constantine Ramses. She was my grandpa's first and only girlfriend. I don't know how faithful he was to her, but that ain't none of my business. The way they still love each other is so sweet.

I knocked on the door and my grandpa cracked open the door and peeked out. He was looking at me like I was interrupting something.

"Dang, Pawpaw, why you answering the door like that for? You don't want any company or something?" I asked him, grinning.

"Oh, boy, I was just getting ready to give your grandmother a massage," he whispered and winked.

"Dear God, Pawpaw. Kill the visual."

"Move, Dane. Come on in here, Duke," my grandmother said, moving my grandpa out the way.

I walked in the door, and along the wall were pictures of me and my brothers. There were all the pictures of me that I have sent from the States. It's like she didn't throw away anything. There was a picture of me and Edwina on the day I left and went to the states. Damn, it's crazy how much time changes things.

"How is everything, grandson? If I wasn't so old, you know I would travel over there to see you and my other grandsons. It's almost time for you to come take over. Are you ready?" Constantine said.

"You're not old, Granny, but I'm about as ready as I'm going to be. Did you know that Edwina was pregnant?"

"Yes, we did, but you don't sound too excited about it. What's the matter? Come have a seat." I went took a seat next to her on the love seat. "Dane, can you grab some of that hot tea off the stove, please?"

My grandpa came in with the tea and sat across from us in his chair. I took one sip of the tea and it tasted amazing. This was one other thing that I missed about living over here: my grandmother's tea. It was so calming.

"I just thought that I was being careful. It seems so fishy to me. You don't think she would try to set me up though, right?"

"Grandson, she is your fiancée. How can she set you up?"

"I don't know. She is carrying my baby and I want to be with her every step of the way, but that is impossible."

"How is that impossible? Just move her to the States."

"NO!" I realized I was yelling. "No, Granny. She can't come to the States."

My grandpa started snickering. He knows me very well. He knows what I got going on in the States. He's also my best friend so I tell him everything, more than I tell my father. She cut her eyes at him, and then back at me.

"Son, are you being the man that you were raised to be?"

"Yes, of course, Granny. Well, I have to go now," I said, cutting the conversation short.

"I bet you do," she said and smacked me upside my head.

I told them that I loved them, and went to my side of the house. Edwina sleeps over here with me when I'm here, but she was still in her other room. So I took the opportunity to get in the shower to wash that long ass plane ride off, and dive in the bed so I could get ready for my long day tomorrow.

In the shower, I turned the jets on high and let the water hit me all over. I closed my eyes and all I saw was her. The same girl that I hate is the same girl that creeps into my mind every time I close my eyes. I grabbed my dick and started stroking it with the thoughts of Pilar's pouty lips going up and down on my shaft.

"Shit," I whispered to myself as I brought myself to a release.

I just need to fuck her one good time, I thought to myself.

I got in the bed and fell asleep.

The next morning I woke up to the roosters calling. I realized that Edwina had slipped her sexy ass in the bed with me. I kissed her on her neck watching her stir in her sleep.

"Good morning, Prince. How did you sleep?"

"I slept okay," I said, knowing damn well I was fucking the shit out of Pilar in my dreams.

"Are you sure? It sounded like you were moaning when I came in here last night."

"It was nothing, babe. I promise."

"Prince, can I ask you a question? I want you to be honest with me."

"Yes, baby."

"Do you have other women over in the States? I know you told me that you are only going to have one wife because that's all you need, but have you changed your mind?"

"No," I replied.

"No to which question, Prince?"

"Figure it out," I replied and went into the bathroom.

I honestly don't know where all this insecurity shit came from with Edwina. This was her first time ever asking me if I had other women in the States. I already told her that I was going to be like my grandpa Dane and have one wife, so the fact that she asked me again bothered me. I put on my work-out clothes because I needed to get in a run. I was going to run around the whole palace twice, and that would bring me to about twenty miles.

"Where are you going?" Edwina asked as soon as I stepped out of the bathroom.

"Where does it look like?" I snapped back and left out the house.

The run was a nice one, and I also did it in a very nice time. My music cut off and my phone started ringing. I answered without looking at the caller ID.

"Speak."

"Sorry… sorry to bother you so late, Mr. Duke, but there is a problem."

I looked at my phone, and it was my bar manager, Frank. He is literally next in line after Brandon. I trust him as well. He knows that he only calls me when he can't get in touch with him.

"It's not late over here. What's going on, Frank?"

"Brandon did not show up to work tonight, and—"

"Wait, run that by me again. Brandon didn't do what?"

I could feel the pressure rising in my head, because I know for sure that I told that bitch ass nigga that he had to be at work this weekend. I didn't give a damn what he and that bitch had planned; his job comes first. When he took the fucking job, I told him that I'm about my business and if he does that job correctly, then he will never have to see another side of me that he doesn't want to see.

"He didn't show up. I called him and he didn't answer. I have left several voicemails, and then all of a sudden, his phone was no longer taking phone calls. The problem is, some woman just came here confronting us about stealing money off of her card. She said this was the last place that her card was used. I mean, I don't have a problem with Brandon not being here, sir, but when things like this arise, he needs to be here. Now this woman is standing at the counter looking like a raging bull. What do I need to tell her?"

"Put her on the phone, please."

"Hello," the woman's voice came over the phone. "What type of fucking place is this? I came here the other night, and then next thing you know, my card has been used to purchase two plane—"

"Good evening, my name is Duke Ramses, and it is my place of business. I'm sorry that this has happened to you and I will make sure that you get reimbursed. I'm going to get to the bottom of this," I spoke into the phone.

I had to cut her off before she got way too mouthy and didn't get shit.

"Yeah, you need to make sure I'm reimbursed plus interest for my trouble before I let everyone know what type of scamming ass place this is."

"Um, Miss, I honestly don't take too kindly to threats so we are going to just stay calm. I will be back in town within the next couple of days, and if you give your direct contact to Frank, I will call you so you can come get the check. Thanks."

"Okay," she said and hung up the phone.

I called Brandon's number, and it said he was not taking calls at the moment. I couldn't even leave a voicemail. I was so fucking pissed. That nigga better consider this shit his fucking resignation.

PILAR

"*P*lease don't be mad at me, Pilar. I said that I was sorry," Brandon said, whispering in my ear.

I ignored him as I looked out the window of my first-class seat. I guess he thinks since he upgraded our seats, I'm supposed to forgive his stupid ass. Brandon and I have been chilling for the last couple of months, and it has been nothing short of awful. We not even together and he has become clingy as shit. He has brought so much unnecessary drama into my life and we are basically friends. I couldn't get rid of him if I tried. When I ignored him, he would pop up at my house or my job. I was not used to this type of shit at all. He literally gets on my damn nerves. I'm one-hundred percent sure that he is sitting next to me on this flight because he thinks I'm going to fuck somebody else in Mississippi, but them niggas are the least of my worries.

"Pilar, please, listen to me," he pleaded.

"I won't listen to you until you tell me who the fuck Veronica is. She made me lose my fucking job, Brandon. She came to my job, claimed she was fucking you, and then proceeded to fight me. Brandon, we are not together, you can tell me the fucking truth. Who is she? I will not ask again," I spat while glaring at him.

I was minding my business at work when some bitch approached me asking me if I was fucking Blizzy. I told her that we could talk after I clocked out, which was going to be within the next thirty minutes, but this bitch swung on me and then missed. I tried to beat that bitch bloody. I may not say much, but I'm definitely not a weak bitch. In Mississippi, you have all the time in the world to learn how to fight because it ain't shit else to do. Not coming from much, like having a crackhead mom and alcoholic grandmother, I had to learn how to fight early because kids were so cruel.

"Alright, listen. She is this girl that I was fucking with before I started fucking with you. That's it. I promise that I ain't fucked with her since I been fucking with you. Pilar, I want to be with you," he pleaded.

I rolled my eyes at his lie. Truth is, I'm a snooper. I can't even lie. I don't trust anybody at all, and the situation that he put me in, is the main reason why. He was in the shower one day, and his phone went off with a series of text messages from Veronica. I read the exchange between them, which let me know that he is dead ass lying to me in my face right now. I literally would have been better off if this was just a one-night stand.

"So, how did you get your boss to let you off this weekend?" I asked, switching subjects.

I needed to change subjects before we messed around and got put off this fucking plane. Swan was supposed to come, but she hates Brandon. When I told her that he was coming, she quickly changed her mind about coming. She told me that something was not right about him.

"I had to beg him. I just wanted to be here with you, Pilar."

"I wouldn't have begged that nigga for anything. You crazy."

"What is the deal with you two? Do y'all have something going on, or had something going on at some point?"

"Brandon, hell fucking no. I didn't even know him until I bumped into him. I regret that day with a passion. He has been a pain in my ass ever since."

I ain't never had a man who gets under my skin the way that Duke's black ass does. He walks around like he's King Tut or somebody. We both piss each other off so bad. I know he be pissed off because his left eye will start twitching and shit. I be catching his punk ass eyes raping me too. When he stares me down, he makes me feel a certain type of way that I would never tell anyone. How can you want somebody to beat the walls off your pussy but hate them at the same time? He's so arrogant, and all the arrogant niggas I have ever fucked with had big dicks. Ruin your life type of big dicks.

"Aw, okay, you better make sure it stays that way," he huffed. "That nigga a big hoe anyway."

"I ain't take you for the type to dirty mack," I said, rolling my eyes and putting my headphones in my ears, not giving him a chance to reply. I could feel him burning a hole in the side of my face, and I was smiling internally.

The whole reason I was even going to Mount Olive was because I wanted to check on Lenora's house and then go put some flowers on their graves. I really didn't have much to miss about Cisco, but I definitely missed Lenora. When the flight landed, Brandon grabbed our bags and we headed to the car rental place. I texted Swan to let her know that I had made it safely, and that I would call her later once I was settled in the hotel. While Brandon was over there talking to the rental car people, my phone started ringing with an unknown number.

"Hello," I answered.

"Bitch, where is Brandon?" the caller said.

I knew that voice. It was the same voice that has been getting on my nerves for the last couple of months.

"Ugh. I know this stank ass accent anywhere. How did you get this number?"

"Don't fucking worry about it. Where the fuck is Brandon? Don't let me fucking ask again or I swear—"

I hung up the phone because Brandon was walking back over. He asked me who I was on the phone with and I told him that it was Swan. I don't even know why I lied to him and I didn't have to. This time my phone went off and I had a text message.

Unknown: I swear to your fucking god, you better tell your fucking boyfriend to find a way to communicate with me or it's going to be his ass the next time I see him.

Me: This is MY phone. If Brandon wanted to communicate with you, then he would, but I will see what I can do. Please don't text me anymore. Thanks in advance.

Unknown: Bitch!

Me: Fuck Boy!

We were on our way to the hotel and I decided to break the

silence.

"Have you gotten in contact with your stupid ass boss since you landed?" I asked him out of curiosity.

"Pilar, I told you that I talked to him before we left. There is no reason for me to be talking to him right now," he said not taking his eyes off the road.

Brandon was lying to me, once again. If it ain't about his whereabouts, or who he talking to, it's something as simple as this. Something ain't right with this nigga, and I swear when we get back to Jacksonville, I'm breaking it off with him. He always talks about how he wants to move into an actual relationship, but he can't even be honest with me while we are simply just friends. We rode the rest of the way in silence. It was a good thing that the ride from Jackson to Mount Olive wasn't long.

When we checked into the hotel, the first thing that I wanted to do was dive in the bed to get some much-needed rest. While Brandon was in the shower, his phone started going off again. I listened to the running water, and I grabbed his phone. I pulled the screen down and I saw the many messages from Duke and some from other bitches asking him how much money he needs and shit. Who the fuck is this nigga? He ain't never asked me for no money. I would slap fire from his ass if he ever did. Duke's messages were basically asking him has he been stealing from the company, and if he had a gambling addiction. The rest of the messages were telling him to call him back immediately. My eyes gawked at the series of questions that Duke was asking. I couldn't put my finger on it at first, but Duke just laid it all out for me and he didn't even know it.

One night I went to his car to look for some lipstick that may have fallen out of my purse and under the seat. I looked under the seat, and there were so many scratch off tickets. Like, if I had counted them it probably would have been about a hundred. I never thought anything about it because I play the scratch off sometimes too, especially since I worked at the damn gas station. I thought that maybe it was just leftovers from a long period of time. My mind was spinning so much that I completely forgot to listen for the water.

"Pilar, what are you doing?" he asked. His voice startled me and I literally dropped his phone, damn near breaking it. "Why were you going through my phone?"

"Honestly, because it kept going off and I wanted to see who kept calling and texting you."

"Uh huh, did you find everything that you were looking for?" he asked me. His voice sounded so scary.

"I know that you are a liar. I know that you still talking to other bitches."

"Pilar, you not trying to be my bitch, so what the fuck you want me to do? You always throwing how 'we not together' in my face, but when I talk to other bitches, you always have a fucking problem. You need to check yourself. You don't want to be in a relationship with me but you don't want me to talk to other bitches. I just can't with you, Pilar. I just want to be with you, and you fucking tripping."

Now, if I was weak ass bitch, I wouldn't have recognized that this nigga was trying to spin this around on me to make me feel bad. I don't know why Brandon hasn't figured out that I'm not the average bitch.

"You just want to be with me and I'm fucking tripping." I reiterated what he said while laughing.

"See, Pilar, you think everything is fucking funny."

"Brandon, just leave. Go back to Jacksonville and I'll talk to you when I get back."

"Ohhh, I see. This was your fucking plan all along, huh? You want to fake argue with me so you can leave and fuck with these niggas around here, huh? I ain't going no fucking where. If you don't want me fucking with bitches, then you ain't about to be fucking with no niggas. Point blank."

I rolled my eyes at him and got in the bed. As soon as my head hit the pillow, I was out like a light.

The next morning came fast. I got up, took care of my morning hygiene, and got dressed. Brandon was still fast asleep. I fished in his pockets looking for the keys to the car. I pulled out a casino chip. I shook my head because he had a problem. I thought I heard the door open and close last night. He drove damn near an hour to the nearest casino. I shook my head at him. I grabbed my things and left out the hotel, leaving him in the bed sleep.

I drove to the nearest Walmart, and got some of those cheap flowers. I had to be careful with my spending since I had just lost my job. I pulled up to the cemetery and got out. Walking towards their graves, I saw a figure standing there. When I got closer, I realized who it was. I know that knock-kneed stance from anywhere. I took a deep breath because I didn't know how this was going to go. Today was

Cisco's birthday and also the day that Lenora died, so I decided I could just kill two birds with one stone. I wanted to give him his privacy so I stopped walking. I was looking at my phone when his voice startled me.

"I loved your mother PP," he said flatly.

I looked up, and he was still looking at the headstone. I wondered how he knew I was standing here.

"Don't call me that!" I quickly retorted, ignoring the statement about my mother.

"Pilar, you may or may not believe me, but I wanted to be in your life. I made several bad decisions in my life, which prevented me from doing that. Pilar, I remember the day that you were born. I was there. You were so tiny but once they found out you had drugs in your system, they called the police. I had to leave because I would have gone to jail as well."

"Because God forbid your uptight ass parents found out what their son was really up to. Prince Harrison, I'm twenty-four years old. I grew tired of your excuses by the time I was ten. I'm completely over you. Finish whatever you were saying so I can put my flowers down and go."

"You wouldn't understand—"

"Oh, I understand perfectly to be exact. Let me tell you exactly what I understand. I understand that you are a coward ass nigga. I understand that you got an underage girl pregnant, got her addicted to crack, and left her to figure things out by herself until she took herself out. I understand that you left a sixty-year-old woman to care for a child, by herself. I understand that you are a selfish bastard, who doesn't even deserve to be standing on Cisco's grave."

"Pilar—"

"NO! It's my time to speak. I understand that you left me here alone, to figure out this world alone. Prince Harrison, do you know how hard it is to have a relationship with a man when the first man in your life let you down? It is because of you that I am unable to love a man fully. All I know about men, is that they get you addicted to crack and leave you stranded with a baby. I have been through dozens of men trying to figure them out, but I just can't. It's because of you that I am an angry black woman. My life is completely fucked up because of you and you don't seem to care. You never cared."

I was too angry because I could feel my face burning, which means it was bloodshot red. My chest was heaving up and down. I was so angry that I probably would have shot him if I had a gun.

"Pilar, can we start over?" He turned and looked at me.

I shook my head because I have heard this all before. He does this every time. He will say he wants to start over and then I won't hear from again for another six months. I rolled my eyes at him. He gave me a card with his name and number on it and he walked away. I waited until he was out of sight before I sat Indian style in between both of their graves.

"Sorry that you guys had to hear that, but that's how I felt. I'm sick of him waltzing in and out of my life. I would much rather him stay gone. I'm barely making it in Jacksonville, but I would rather stay there than come back here any day. I'm going to find me another job soon.

I hope that job that Swan was talking about comes through, because I really need it. I hope you guys continue to rest well. I will be back next year," I said.

I put the flowers on their graves and then headed to the car. I drove down my old street and then pulled up to the house that I grew up in. It was still in the same shape that it was when I left. I pulled my key out and went inside. It was just as I left it. Swan's parents had a maid service to come clean up really good in here right after she died. I didn't take anything from here because none of it was useful at all. I went down in the storage area and turned the light on. It wasn't much in here but a bunch of boxes full of shit. Lenora never threw anything away.

None of their clothes were useful because they were all so smoked out, so I threw all of them away. They were too fucked up to even take to a Goodwill. I found a box that had nothing but picture albums in it. I loved to look at pictures, even though I barely took them once I got older. These picture albums are coming with me. I never really had any toys because they couldn't afford them. There was basically a brand-new bike in the corner. Prince Harrison got me that bike for my tenth birthday, and I never even rode it. That's just how much hatred I had in my heart for that man. That is something that I can take to the Goodwill. When I got closer to the door, there was a small hole in the wall with something sticking out. I moved the cobwebs out of the way and got the box out. I didn't open it, but I put it in the box of photo albums that I was going to take with me.

I looked in each of the rooms, and they still looked the same as I left them. This house was a small, two-bedroom, one-bathroom home. I was actually surprised that none of those hoodlum-ass kids broke in here and turned it into a trap house, or whatever it is that they are doing down here now. I put the things that I was taking with me, in the car, took one last look at the house then drove off. In a few months, I'll have Swan's mom to swing by and check on it.

After dropping that bike off at the Goodwill, I headed back to the hotel. My phone started ringing and Brandon's name came across the screen. I didn't answer it because I was on my way back to the hotel anyway. The phone rang again, and I answered not looking at the caller ID.

"WHAT!" I shouted into the phone.

"Put Brandon on the phone, bitch!" he shouted into the phone.

"Fuck boy! Brandon is not around me. I left him at the hotel. His phone is working, because he just called me. Bye."

"Don't hang up," he said in a much calmer voice.

I hung up anyway because he gets on my damn nerves, and I didn't want to hear anything else that he was talking about. When I made it back to the hotel, Brandon was up pacing the room.

"Pilar, you're okay!" He rushed over to me and started hugging and kissing all over me.

"Brandon, get your hands off of me. I'm fine. What is wrong with you? You finally woke up and you thought that I left your ass? I should have, but I didn't. I just took care of everything that I came to take care of."

"Why didn't you wake me?"

"I didn't want to. I'm sure you needed the rest after last night's activities."

"I couldn't sleep."

"You couldn't sleep, so you decided to drive an hour to the nearest casino and play. Brandon, you have a problem and you need to get help for it."

"I know, Pilar." He sighed and laid back on the bed.

"Another thing… wait, what did you say?"

"I know I need help. I was doing fine and then all of a sudden it just came back. The urges and shit just came back out of nowhere."

"Are you admitting that you have a gambling problem?"

"Yes, I guess I am, Pilar."

I didn't know what else to say after that because I wasn't expecting him to flat out admit that he had a gambling problem. He proceeded to tell me about his family, their problems, and how he gets it honestly. He told me about everything, except his womanizing ass ways. I didn't say anything else to him and we headed to the airport in silence. He kept asking me if I was mad at him but I wasn't. I just wanted to get back to Jacksonville so I could delete and block him from my life.

BRANDON

I hadn't talked to Pilar since we came back from Mississippi. I know I fucked up when I left her in the bed and went to gamble, but I couldn't help it. She didn't know this, but I legit was having deep ass feelings for her. But as much as I like her, I loved different pussy and gambling more. As soon as I touched down, I went and spoke to Duke. That nigga broke my nose in three different places, and told me if I ever tried some shit like that again he would kill me. He let me keep my job though. You think that would have been enough for me to stop stealing from him and gambling, but it wasn't. At least he didn't know that I had a problem. All he knew was that I didn't come to work when he asked me to.

See, there is a machine that you can get from Amazon for like twenty dollars that reads credit card information if they are within five to ten feet of you. So, every night I go to work, I put the machine in my suit jacket, and catch about twenty to thirty cards a night. I go home and make duplicate cards, and I max them shits out so fast, and then throw them away. I know a nigga could easily be doing something else with his time, getting shit legally, but that takes too long. I'm a 'right now' kind of nigga. At first it was easy to steal from Duke because he trusted me, so I had all the codes to everything. I was taking about five thousand every other day out of his safe. I mean, this nigga was a millionaire. He could wipe his ass with five thousand dollars. After he broke my nose, he changed all the codes and shit. Now he made shit harder, but it was still doable. I know I shouldn't be stealing from the very person who gave me a job, but like they say, money is the root of all evil.

"You ready to eat, Blizz?" Veronica asked.

Veronica was this chick I had been messing around with since high school. She has always been the one that I can come back to, regardless of what I do. I thought she was legit done with me when Pilar beat her ass, but she kept calling me telling me how sorry she was for doing that. Back in high school, she used to beat every girl up that I fucked with then they would stop fucking with me. The only girl that has ever whooped her ass was Pilar. Veronica told me that she didn't care that I fucked with Pilar. She just wanted me to fuck with her too. Bitches are funny as hell, man.

"Sure," I replied.

She brought out a plate of neckbones, greens, sweet potatoes, and cornbread. Come to think of it, Pilar never cooked for me; but a part of me still missed her a little. I would text her but she would not reply. Every time I went by her house that bitch Swan always said that was gone when I knew that was a lie. Hell, Pilar didn't even have a damn car, nor did she work.

"What's wrong, Blizz?"

"Not shit, really. I'm just trying to relax before I have to go to work, that's all."

"Why are you still working for him, especially after he broke your damn nose?"

"Well, I will quit and let you pay all my bills."

"You acting like that's far-fetched now."

I cut my eyes at her, letting her know that she needed to shut the fuck up. I know I'm a scammer and a womanizer, but I hate when it comes out of other people's mouth. I finished eating in silence because if I would have responded to that, it would have started an argument that I didn't even feel like having. I went into the room and pulled out my suit for tonight. This was a big night because we were having some local rappers come in and showcase their talents tonight, so I had to be dapper. I know the women are going to be out in abundance tonight.

I looked myself up and down in the mirror and approved of the midnight blue, tailored Versace suit, with a white button down. I paired it with a black bowtie and black Versace shoes. Yeah, your boy was fly as shit. I went and got my hair lined up earlier today which had me feeling myself. I had my one-karat studs in my ear, blinging. My whole ensemble tonight came close to fifteen thousand dollars, all courtesy of Duke. Man, I'm going to get so many fucking numbers tonight. I can feel that shit. I laughed to myself because a nigga was legit sick with the scamming. I'm going to get just a little more and I swear I'mma be done. Tonight was going to do numbers so it was going to be the perfect night.

When I walked out the room, Veronica had on her all black bodycon dress, paired with some black red bottoms. I got them for her birthday last year. I'm a fucked up individual, but not that fucked up.

She was standing in the mirror putting the finishing touches on her makeup. Me, personally, I didn't think she needed that shit. She had pretty chocolate skin that glowed when she was happy and when I was putting this dick to her. Her body was even stacked nicely even though she had a little pudge.

"I'm riding with you," she said. "Stop staring at me. You like what you see?"

I honestly don't even remember telling Veronica she could go. It was going to be hard to move the way I wanted to with her there, but how I could say no when she was already dressed up.

"You know I always like what I see."

"Brandon, you ain't gon' be acting funny or nothing with me when we get there, right? What if that curly hair bitch there?"

"Veronica, you are asking too many questions, babe. Just finish getting ready because I don't want to be late."

I didn't answer her question because I was going to be trying my best to avoid her tonight, especially if I wanted to get a lot of bitches. You know how bitches are when they go somewhere with their niggas and a lot of women be there. They be all over you like they trying to make them all jealous or some shit. That gets annoying. Pilar didn't do any of that shit. That weird mothafucka barely even liked public displays of affection. I don't know who hurt her, but she was a tough onion to peel. I knew for a fact that Pilar was not going to be there because she hates Duke and she doesn't talk to me anymore. She really doesn't have a reason to be there, but if she just so happens to be there, I am going to try and talk to her.

"I'm going to the car, V," I hollered out and then went and sat in the car.

I pulled my phone out and checked my bank accounts. This has always been a habit of mine. In my savings account, there was thirty thousand dollars, and in fifteen in my checking account. I had another account that I used for my gambling addiction. I put two thousand dollars a month in it and I tried to stay within that limit; but when I checked it, it was in the negative. It was only the middle of the month, and I had like fifteen more days before the two thousand dollars went into that account. I don't know how I'm going to make it.

"Brandon, you can do this," I said to myself, and closed out my accounts.

"You can do what?" Veronica asked, getting into the car.

"Nothing."

When we pulled up to Duke's, the mothafuckin' line was around the corner. There were crowds of people waiting to get in and I just knew that it was about to go down tonight. I went around back and parked in my parking spot. Duke's Lamborghini was parked in its spot. I didn't expect him to be here so early. It's crazy because he is the only person I knew who had a four hundred-thousand-dollar car as his every day car. This nigga is flashy as shit, and I ain't never heard about this nigga being robbed or some shit. This nigga really be rolling through Duval County with the top back, like he ain't driving this mothafucka. If I didn't know this nigga, I would have been stuck this nigga up and stole his car or some shit.

Veronica and I went through the back door and I didn't hear any music playing, which was weird. When I went out on the floor, no one was in there. The people at the bar were there but that's it.

"Where is Frank?" I asked one of the girls. "Why is everybody waiting outside?"

"You might want to go see Duke, Mr. Lewis," Frank said from behind me.

I turned and looked at him and he had a look of worry on his face. I was kind of scared because for a split-second, I thought that he may have figured out that I was stealing from him, but he couldn't have known that shit. I talked to him this morning and he was sounding like his normal self. There is nothing that I could have done wrong. I left Veronica downstairs at the bar while I went to deal with Duke. I knocked on his door and he told me to come in. When I walked in, there were three white dudes standing there with him.

"Brandon, I'm going to ask you this one time and one time only. It'll be in your best interest not to lie to me. Before I thrash these white niggas for coming in here lying to me, you paid the building permits? Please say yes, so I won't look like a fool in front of these people that's in here trying to shut my shit down," he said so low and menacing.

Shit, I thought to myself. I knew it was something that I was supposed to do with that money that Duke gave me. Damn, he gave me that shit two months ago. The minute he put that money in my hand, I went straight to the casino. I thought that I would have remembered to go pay them crackers, and the shit slipped my mind.

"BRANDON!" he yelled and slammed his hand down on the desk, scaring me so bad that I farted a little.

"Boss, let me explain—"

He held his hand up, cutting me off.

"Gentlemen, I am so sorry. Please let me—"

"I have the cash in my account. If you can just take the payment tomorrow morning when I go to the bank," I cut Duke off.

"You have fifteen thousand dollars just laying around in your account, Brandon?" he asked me, clasping his hands on his stomach, and leaning back in his seat.

"I thought it was just five thousand! When did it become fifteen thousand?"

"Well, when you don't pay your bills on time, there is something called late and interest fees, but that's okay, Brandon, because I got it from here," he said smiling.

"Gentlemen, I am going to pay you right now, if I can. Shutting down tonight is going to cost me so much money, and I can't stand to lose the money tonight. I have several people performing that I have to pay," Duke pleaded.

"Since there was a little bit of communication problems on your end, then we will let you pay us tonight, in cash or by a check."

Duke glared at me, and I looked away because there was nothing that I could say that would even make him feel better about this shit. He turned around and opened the safe. He typed the code so fast that I missed it. He counted out fifteen stacks for the men. They collected their money and left out quickly.

"Duke—"

He held up his hand.

"I didn't say that you could speak, Brandon."

He got on the phone and called downstairs to Frank, to let him know that he could start letting people in. I felt the vibrations through the wall as the music came alive.

"You looking very dapper tonight. I know Versace when I see it. I purchased two of those same suits about a week ago. I'm sure that particular one ran for about five thousand alone. Is that where my money went to? The money that I gave you to pay for the building permit."

"Nigga, you act like I'm working for you for free. You pay me."

"You're deflecting. The question I asked you requires a yes or a no, not an explanation."

"No."

"Soooo, where did the money go? How could you have forgotten to go pay them, when that was supposed to be your first stop as soon as I put the money in your hand? What did you do in between the time that I gave you the money and the time that you were supposed to go pay them? I have so many questions, Brandon; you better start talking," Duke spat.

He opened both of his drawers, pulling a pistol out of each one. I watched him take the safety off of both of them. I ain't never been so afraid for my life. I didn't even know what to tell him. I felt like I was in a lose-lose situation. If I told him the truth, which was that I gambled it away, he would shoot me. If I lied, he would be able to tell, and he would definitely shoot me.

"Um, let me explain. When I was younger—"

"I absolutely don't have that type of time. Short, sweet, to the point."

I went ahead and told him that I had a gambling problem. I told him that I had stopped at the casino and gambled the money away. I also told him that I thought I would have remembered to go pay them when I got paid, but it slipped my mind. I said everything in one big breath too. I didn't know what he was going to say, but he just got quiet and stared at me. It was one of those deathly quiet stares, where you didn't know what was going to happen.

"Ten years of friendship, and I never knew this about you," he said, shaking his head.

Now that I think about this shit, we have been friends for ten years, and I don't know a lot of shit about him either. Hell, I ain't never been in this nigga's house. I'd only been in the driveway, and that's because he had forgot something at home. I don't even think that we can consider ourselves best friends. We are more business partners than anything.

"Brandon, you put my business in jeopardy because of your stupidity and addiction. Make this... what the fuck?" he said, raising up and looking at the monitor in front of him.

"We have to get downstairs."

I don't know what was happening, but I was glad that it stopped him from saying whatever he was going to say.

PILAR

I have felt so free since I blocked Brandon's ass. I am really weird, but I hate relationships. I'm so selfish with my time and space that I don't ever see myself being in a healthy relationship. The times that Brandon slept over, I literally could not sleep at all. I hated to have to share my bed with him. I swear to God, the closest person I have to a boyfriend is Swan. She legit knows everything about me.

Today, I spent all day filling out job applications. I was filling out job applications everywhere. Hell, I even took the bus to Love's to practically beg for my job back, but the manager said no. Even after Lee and I told her that the bitch came in there and started with me. Lee told the manager that I offered to talk to her after I clocked out, but that didn't even work. I wasted a bus ride, so I just sat on the bench and started thinking about my life.

"Ms. Pilar, where you been, girl?" Charlie came and sat next to me. "I haven't seen you in months."

"Well, you know I was talking to that boy that pulled up that night. He had been picking me up as soon as eleven hit. I used to try and wait around on you but he would rush me out the store. For some odd reason, he was jealous of you. You know that night in the car he gave me the third degree about you? That was the funniest thing, but he was right about one thing regarding you."

"What is that?"

"I legit don't know anything about you but the fact that you're homeless. You're always listening to me talk."

"Well, that's how you get to know people, ain't it?"

"Yeah, you're right, but anyways… that guy and I are cancelled. He was too clingy and he has too many issues that I ain't willing to deal with. I'm not relationship material and I have come to terms with that."

"Everybody is relationship material. You just haven't met the right guy yet. Keep living. You're not that old. Why are you not in uniform? You're not working today?"

"Oh, I got fired. That was one of the issues that he had. He was a big hoe, and some bitch came to my job and fought me. Her name was Veronica. I tried to kill her since I knew I was going to lose my job anyway. It was a good thing the manager didn't call the police because I would have gone to jail and spent I don't know how many days."

"You are going to be alright, Pilar. You are much smarter than you give yourself credit for. How long are you going to be sitting here?"

"I don't have shit else to do. I came down here to see if I could get my job back, but after begging and pleading, she said no. So I'm going to wait until the next bus comes and go back home."

"Let me walk you there."

We walked to the bus stop in silence. He stayed with me until the bus came. Once I got on the bus, I laughed to myself because he once again skated away without telling me nothing about himself. When I got home, I walked in on Swan getting piped down by Brian. They were fucking on the living room couch. He tried to stop, but she kept throwing it back on him.

"Hey, y'all," I spoke, like it was normal for me to see it.

"Hmmm, heyyy, bitch," Swan moaned out.

I went in my room and put my headphones in to drown out Swan's moans, and then I fell asleep. I was sleeping good until I felt some cold hands on my breasts. I jumped awake.

"Bitch, get up. We going out. We are going to Duke's. Some new artists are supposed to be performing. You know it's going to be live as shit."

"No, no, and no. Brandon and his stupid ass boss is going to be there. I don't have the time or energy to deal with them both."

"Bitch, fuck them. If I ain't know any better I would say that you were feeling his boss, because you always talking about him."

"I probably only mentioned him once or twice. No more than five times," I said, trying to remember how many times I had actually mentioned him to Swan.

"Exactly, which is more times than you have ever talked about Brandon's stupid ass."

"Whatever. You better be glad I love you."

I got ready in record time. I showered and put on a gray bodycon dress, with a pair of Rhianna's burgundy Creepers. I liked this dress because it showed some major side boob. The line wasn't as long as it was the first time we had to stand in it. When we made it inside, it was packed as hell like it was last time. We went to back of the building where the stage was because some group was getting ready to perform. I looked over in the corner and saw that bitch.

"Girl, that's the bitch that I fought, Veronica," I yelled over the music in Swan's ear.

"Bitch, where, because I'm about to beat her mothafuckin' ass."

"Swan, don't do this," I said, grabbing her arm, trying to stop her.

"Move, Pilar. She made you lose your fucking job. That shit does not fly with me."

Swan broke away from me and approached Veronica. She backed up against the wall.

"So you the bitch that made my bitch lose her job, and over a fuck ass nigga!" Swan yelled, pointing her finger in her face.

"Get your finger out my face, hoe. Brandon is my mothafuckin' nigga. That nigga just spent the night with me last night. I don't care about that hoe losing her—"

"Wrong choice of words!" Swan yelled.

That bitch was getting ready to say that she didn't care about me losing my job and I snapped. I just started swinging on her ass like my mothafuckin' life depended on it. I don't play about my money. I didn't expect Swan to jump in though. This was just like old times, when we used to jump bitches at college parties for being disrespectful. She was on the ground trying to block our kicks. We were going in on her ass until somebody yanked me and Swan up and started dragging our ass to the front. My fucking titties were out and everything. I could only cover them a little bit.

"Drop them," I heard the annoying accent.

The man dropped us so fast, and then I was able to fix myself.

"Pilar, what the fuck is your problem?" Brandon asked, standing over me. "This is my fucking job, and you bring this shit to my job."

"Brandon, shut the fuck up," I said, getting up off the floor. "I wouldn't have beat that bitch ass if she hadn't of said that she didn't give a damn about me losing my job. You better pawn that fake ass watch and get her teeth fixed," I spat.

"And before your stupid ass say anything, I am getting THE FUCK out of your establishment," I spat to Duke.

"I'm glad you knew what the fuck to do," he said to Swan's and my back.

"Why you always got to get the last fucking word in? You make me so fuckin' sick," I turned and got in his face.

My adrenaline was on a thousand already. I don't even know why I was in this big ass man's face like I could actually beat his ass. I could feel my face burning and his left eye was twitching. He was getting ready to say something, but Swan had pulled me away.

"Come on, girl, before that man beat your ass in here," Swan said.

"I'mma deal with your ass later, Pilar!" Brandon yelled at our backs.

When we got outside, we both fell out laughing at the same time. I'm sure we were both thinking the same thing.

"Biiitttccchhh, was that Duke? If so, I see why your ass is in love with him. That's who you should have fucked with instead of Brandon's dumb, broke ass."

"I am not in love with Duke. I hate him, actually. We have never even had a civil conversation. That exchange back there is definitely the premise of whatever relationship you think we got going on."

"Pilar, shut the fuck up. I watched that exchange, and all I saw was two people who want to fuck the living daylights out of each other. That nigga's dick was starting to stand up in his damn slacks. You know I'm watching prints, and I can tell you that he is much bigger than Brandon. Bitch, fuck that nigga and get it over with. That shit is inevitable, and he's going to be the one that makes you finally cum. Trust me."

I rolled my eyes and slightly gagged at the thought of even fucking Duke. At times, I hated that Swan knew so much of my business because she doesn't care when she blurts it out... like now. I didn't want to be reminded that my body doesn't have orgasms during intercourse. We rode the rest of the way in silence. I just wanted to go get back in the bed and sleep for the rest of my life.

DUKE

*T*he longer she stood in front of me, the harder my dick was starting to get. I was so glad when her friend pulled her away because if she hadn't, I would have had precum all over the front of my slacks. When they walked away, I took a deep breath and told Brandon that we were not done, and he was still needed in my office. He had a look of death on his face. Little did he know, I would not kill him in my office, because my carpet cost me twenty thousand dollars, and I wouldn't dare mess it up with blood. Blood wouldn't come out of this carpet, and I didn't want to buy a new one. I kicked back and played back the fight. They beat the fuck out of that girl. I did hear Pilar say that the girl made her lose her job. I shook my head because I legit thought that Brandon had feelings for Pilar and had put his hoeish ways behind him, but I was wrong.

"Duke, I swear that shit won't happen again. I'mma handle Pilar for that weak ass shit that her and Swan did," he said, rushing in my office.

"I honestly don't care about that. I care more about my money, and the misuse of it. You told me about your addiction, and I know how hard it was as a man for you to tell me that, but Brandon, I no longer need your services. I will give you a healthy severance package, and I will pay for any rehab of your choice. That is the very least that I can do, because I could kill you."

He stood there like he was still trying to process what I said.

"Oh, and if you're wondering, this is the end of our friendship as well. You stole from me and almost made my shit get shut down. If you haven't learned anything about me within these last ten years, I am all about my business. Coming in between me and my business has serious consequences, and this is one of them."

"It… it was just one small thing," he finally stuttered.

"It's funny that you consider that *one small thing* because had they shut this building down, I would have easily lost out on three hundred grand tonight. Do you have three hundred grand to spare, Brandon?"

He shook his head.

"I thought so. So, if there isn't anything else, then you are dismissed," I said and kicked back. "Oh, and stop by the bar to grab your last check and severance package from Frank."

He didn't say anything as he walked out of my office. I didn't feel sorry for his ass at all, because he fucked with the right one. I went back to scanning the monitor, so I could see who I could take home tonight. I didn't want to call any of my old hoes, even though they would be delighted to meet me at my loft downtown. Once I spotted who I would be taking home with me, I sent one of my boys to go get her name and number. I never did any of that type of shit. I wouldn't be caught dead talking to any of these hoes. I watched on the monitor as one of my boys went and whispered in her ear. I zoomed in on her smiling ass. Ten minutes later, there was a knock on the door.

"Hey, boss. Her name is Takiya Mowry, and she said that she would love to accompany you for a nightcap. I gave her the address to the loft, and she said that she will meet you there," Goldman said, standing at the door.

"Okay, good. Does she understand that sex will be had at this nightcap?"

"Yes, boss, she said she understood. Another thing, I heard about what happened with Brandon. How soon are you looking to replace him?"

"You know somebody?" I asked him

He cleared his throat and then smiled. I raised my eyebrow at him because I wanted him to actually say what he was thinking.

"Me. I would like to apply for the position. I'm not trying to brag or anything, but I would like to think that I was more qualified than him anyway to begin with. I know you were just trying to be nice when you let him get that high ass position in this business," he said, smirking.

He was right. I knew that Brandon wasn't qualified to do something like this, but since we had some type of friendship established, I thought I was just doing the right thing. Sometimes, the people that you try to help are the same people that will bring you down, and not have a fucking care in the world.

"Well, we will see what happens. Put in your application and then we will go from there. How does that sound?"

"I will do just that." He nodded his head and shut the door.

I knew that I was going to hire him for the position, but I still needed to be formal about things. I opened up my computer and went into my private tracker. I typed in Takiya's name, and hacked into her medical records from every medical facility she had ever been to. I looked over her medical records to make sure that she ain't never had no shit that she couldn't get rid of. I'm usually a good judge of character when I pick out women. I was happy that she ain't have shit, even though I was going to use a rubber anyway.

For the sake of curiosity, I typed in Pilar's name. Her medical records came up clean for any type of sexual transmitted diseases, but I saw that she was on Valium and Zoloft. She been on that shit since she was in high school. I added another screen and looked up those medications. Valium is mainly used for anxiety, and Zoloft is used for anger. It seems like both of these medications are used for the same thing, so I wonder why she is taking both, or even if she is taking both of them. This girl is very interesting… very, very interesting. I saw that her last refill was a year ago, for a three-month supply. She is probably out of medications, which is probably where her anger comes from. I heard Frank call out for last call at the bar, so I decided to exit out the computer and leave. I hated the traffic on this side of town when all of the clubs closed.

Heading to my car, I called Mariah to let her know that I was going to the loft. She knows that when I go to the loft that she needs to bring over a package for the young lady for when she leaves. She told me that she would come drop it off in a few hours. As soon as I made it to the loft, I jumped in the shower. Thirty minutes later, I heard a soft knock on the door.

"Come in," I said.

When she walked in, she was looking shy and shit.

"Well, hello. Come on in, I don't bite…hard. Go take a shower for me, and there is a complimentary robe for you when you get out. Would you like something to drink?"

She smiled while nodding her head.

"Do you have something fruity, like a daiquiri or a sangria? I love those," she said, smiling.

Damn, I done it again. I picked out a nice ass redbone. I watched her walk to the bathroom, and her ass was thick as hell. She wasn't a fat girl, but she wasn't a skinny girl either. She had to be like a size twelve, and with her being short, it made her look even more stacked. She had on this tight ass dress, and her ass jiggled every time she walked. My dick got hard just thinking about, how that ass was going to be twerking on this dick. While she showered, I fixed her drink.

I was sitting in my chair, nursing my Hennessy on the rocks, when she walked in the living room. I liked for my women to have a really clean smell, so I kept some Dove soap in the bathroom for them to use. She sat on the couch across from me, next to her drink. She took one sip, and I saw her eyes close. It was like she had tasted one of the best drinks in the world.

"This tastes good. You made this yourself?" she asked me.

I nodded my head.

"Wow, this tastes exceptionally good. This is better than anything that I have ever had before. I hope that you will make me another drink soon," she said while laughing.

"Ohh, how much alcohol did you put in this?" she asked, grinning.

"Not much," I replied.

I smiled because the Spanish Fly was working. I put two drops in her drink because she was thick. I used Spanish Fly because I wanted the girls to have the best sex experience in their lives. I don't consider this a drug because it only heightens yours senses and increased your libido so you can have mind-blowing orgasms. I love pleasing women, and it gives me great joy knowing that they will never have another experience like fucking with 'The Duke' in their life.

Her eyes were getting low, and she was staring me at me, looking sexy as hell. I slowly opened my robe and let it fall open. My dick was standing at full attention. She looked at it and started biting her lip.

"It's okay, baby, I know you a virgin."

"I'm not a virgin."

"You ain't never had Duke before, baby. You a virgin. Come get on your knees."

She got on her knees and crawled in between my legs, and took my hard ass dick in her mouth. She was sucking on it like her life depended on it. I was trying to get into it, but her head was not good at all. I don't know how to teach bitches how to suck dick because I don't. Shit. I didn't even teach Edwina. I just made her ass watch pornos, and before long, her ass was a pro at it.

"Just relax, baby. This dick ain't going nowhere. Tighten your mouth up a little."

She did what I asked her to do, and it was a little better, but still not good enough for me to get into. I moved her mouth, and she was grinning like she had really did a good job. I pulled out a magnum from my robe pocket, and she shook her head.

"What?"

"I'm allergic to latex," she said quickly.

"That's cool," I replied, pulling out a Trojan Bareskin condom.

I opened it and rolled it down my dick. I scooted down so my ass was on the edge of the seat. She straddled me and slid halfway on my dick, before she got up. She started again, and then slid all the way down on it.

"Dearrr God, this dick is so big," she moaned out.

She started bouncing on my dick like she was riding a horse, surprising the shit out of me. I guess where she lacked in head, she made up in pussy, because this shit was so fucking good. I picked her up and carried her to the guest bedroom. I laid her down on the bed, because I was about to drill the fuck out of this pussy.

"Damn, I ain't never had a man who could pick me up."

"Stop fucking with weak niggas."

I spread her legs as far as they could go, and went deep as I could inside of her. She started moaning like crazy, which was only music to my ears. She started playing with her clit, while I was fucking her. I loved when women did that shit.

"Oooweee, Mr. Duke, baby, I'm finnna cummm," she moaned.

I kept my pace until she creamed my dick up. I flipped her over, pushed her chest in the bed, and started fucking her. I spread her cheeks and started giving her long deep strokes. I closed my eyes and rolled my head back as I continued to stroke her. Looking down, I saw that curly ass hair that I hate so fucking much. I started power driving her. I grabbed both of her arms, holding them behind her, fucking her... hard. She started screaming.

"Mr. Dukkkeeee... Shit, you're hurting this pussy."

I blinked my eyes and came back to reality. I wasn't fucking Pilar. It was just my imagination. I slowed down and pulled out of her. My dick was starting to get soft. I couldn't even finish because my thoughts had gone to her.

"Damn, you fucked me so fucking good," she whispered before she went to sleep.

I left her there in that position, while I went and jumped in the shower. I went to my bedroom where I slept and waited until morning.

"Mr. Duke, what is this?" someone screamed.

I thought I was dreaming. I opened my eyes to see a pissed off Takiya waving a paper around. I already knew what it was, but for the sake of entertaining her, I grabbed it anyways.

"Your majesty, I tried to stop her," Mariah said running in the room behind her out of breath.

"YOUR MAJESTY?" she yelled again. "WHO THE FUCK ARE YOU?"

I groaned at the fact that Mariah had slipped and called me Your

Majesty. I couldn't be too mad at her, because I ain't never had a non-compliant woman before. This is new for me, and her.

"This is a NDA, also known as a Non-disclosure agreement. Once you sign this agreement, you will not speak of anything that happened in this loft last night. You can't discuss anything about me."

"Basically, you don't know me, and I don't know you."

"You said that… not me."

"What if I don't sign this? My sex is worth more than a measly five thousand dollars," she spat, ripping up the check.

"On the contrary… Look, just sign this paper. If you don't sign it… then I force you. I hate to have to get up out of this bed because you don't want to sign a piece of paper. Why you want to go around and talk about the people you have sex with anyway? That's trashy, and very unappealing."

"Well, the people I normally have sex with don't drive expensive ass cars," she said, rolling her neck.

"Alright, look, if I have to get up, I'm going to be so mad. You are cutting into my sleeping time."

"Well give me ten thousand dollars, then."

"There is not a negotiation for this. You either sign this or I have that young man behind you *escort* you to your car. I hope I don't have to go into details what will happen in that parking garage. You have five seconds. Mariah, hand her a pen, please."

She signed that paper so fast.

"You can keep the robe, the soap, and Mariah will give you a copy of your signed agreement on the way out the door. You also need to work on your head game. Your pussy got really wet, but it was also subpar. You might want to clench those muscles during the day while you ain't doing shit," I said, and turned over and went back to sleep.

I wasn't even sleep for long, before I felt that someone was in the room watching me. I turned over, and my brothers were staring at me, along with my accountant, Richard Slater.

"What did I miss?" I asked them as they all stared at me.

"We got you your evidence," Baron said.

"Brandon's already fired. That's the end of that."

"Nah, bro, you might want to see this, for real," Baron said.

For the next ten minutes, I listened to how they found out that Brandon had been stealing from me. They had it laid all out. This nigga was stealing out of my safe and changing Richard's paperwork in the computer. I trusted Richard with my money, so I trusted that he would count it and not steal from me. Richard said that he found out that he was changing it because he wrote the numbers down in a book, and he realized that the computer was changed but the book was different. No one else would have a reason to steal from me. My feelings were legit hurt from hearing that shit.

"So, how much have he stole approximately?" I asked, rubbing my temples.

I had to fire up the blunt because I had legit just gotten mad. I paid this man good as hell, and for him to steal from me pissed me the fuck off. I was legit scared to ask this question because I might flip my mothafuckin' wig if it's a wild ass amount.

"Um, fifty thousand dollars, sir."

I closed my eyes because I legit had gotten light headed. We had barely been open for six months. How the fuck was he able to get fifty thousand dollars away from me?

"How much did you say?" I asked Richard again for dramatic effect.

"Sir, fifty—"

I raised my hand up to stop him. I just couldn't hear the number again.

"That's…that's not all, bro. You might want to hit the blunt for this shit," Bomani, my baby brother advised.

I took two pulls off the blunt before they finished the story.

"He had been stealing from customers as well. Over the last couple of weeks, I have been meeting women and placing them strategically where I know Brandon would stop and talk to them. Those same women would call me later in the week and tell me that their card was used for large amounts. I put two and two together and the common denominator was him. He has to have some type of machine that scans their credit cards. He then goes and maxes them out. Bro, I told your ass something wasn't right about that nigga," Baron said, showing me pictures of the camera, and Brandon interacting with those women.

"Have those women been compensated?" I asked no one in particular.

"Yes, they have been compensated. I made sure of that," Baron said.

I just got real quiet for a minute. There's nothing more that I hate than a thief. I mean I'm an asshole, but if you need the shirt off my back then I will give it to you. I felt the knife in my back turning. Fifty thousand dollars. That's basically chump change because I make more than that in one night, almost ten times that with all my locations. He could have asked for that.

"So, what do we do now?" Baron asked.

"You know what to do… kill him," I said and laid back down on the bed.

Richard's white ass was looking pale in the face. He gon' find out how the Ramses brothers get down. You don't fuckin' take from me. You take from me, I take your life. End. Of. Discussion.

BRANDON

I been chilling for the last two weeks, but I was legit pissed when Duke fired me. He offered to pay for any type of rehab that I would go to, but I ain't going to no fucking rehab, not for no gambling. I ain't even know they had this shit, until I was sitting here looking on my phone. It was expensive as hell, and I was not about to spend thirty thousand dollars. A thousand dollars a day just to sit up and discuss how gambling has ruined my life. Nah, I can do that on my fucking own. I can write in a fucking journal on my own.

"Baby, he really fired you because I fought with Pilar? That's fucked up for real," Veronica said, placing the plate down in front of me.

"Yeah, man. I didn't expect shit to go down that way though. Are you alright? Your eye is still a little swollen."

I told her that Duke fired me because of the fight. I didn't want to tell her that he fired me for a completely different reason.

"Yeah, it's okay. That bitch is crazy though. It's like she hit me even harder than when I was in the gas station. I guess it's karma because I made her lose her job. God really doesn't like ugly," she sighed.

I didn't say anything, because I didn't want to have this

conversation. She kept talking anyway.

"Damn, it ain't even like you stole from his ass. I could understand him firing you if you were stealing from him. I hate a thief, but you got fired because of another bitch. Now I want to murk that bitch for real."

I ignored her because she doesn't need to know about that part of my life. She talks so fucking much and this is why I couldn't be with her all the time. I had to make Pilar's little ass talk, but this mothafucka won't shut the fuck up.

"So, what are you going to do now?" she had asked me when I had finally tuned back into the conversation.

"I'll think of something. I'll be back. I'm going to run home right quick, and get some more clothes," I said and left out the door.

I was turning on my street when I saw a car outside in my yard, and I didn't even want to know who that was, so I turned around in the middle of the street and started driving around. At the red light, I pulled out my phone and went to my Facebook. Pilar and I were still friends on there, so I had to message her.

Me: Hey! I know it's been a while, but I really want to talk to you. Can I take you to dinner tonight?

Pilar Renee Harrison: It hasn't been a while, Brandon. It's only been a couple of weeks, since you tried to check me at the pool hall. I hope that bitch eye is still swollen. What you want to talk about, and why you want to take me to dinner? Say what you need to say right here.

Me: I need to get some things off my chest. I want to say it face to face. I want to look into those eyes.

Pilar Renee Harrison: *You have been honest enough.*

Me: *Please.*

Pilar Renee Harrison: *Alright.* Come pick me up at nine. Bye.

I tried to write her back, but I was already blocked. It was a good thing that I had already saved her profile picture. It was so funny because when I looked at Pilar's picture, I saw so much behind her eyes. I went back to Veronica's house and waited for my date with Pilar.

Later that night, I was waiting outside her house at ten minutes before nine. She came out right at nine. She had on one of those dresses that she had on at the pool hall, but this one was black and she had on black Nike shoes. When she got in the car, I saw that she on black lipstick and black fingernail polish. The black cross body bag blended in as well.

"You feeling really gothic tonight, ain't you? This all black is scaring me," I said breaking the ice.

"I felt really dark today for some odd reason," she replied.

We rode the rest of the way to the restaurant in silence. I made us a reservation for late evening at Barbara Jean's restaurant, in Ponte Vedra. It's a small city outside of Jacksonville. It's a little country style restaurant that serves soul food, and I knew that Pilar would love it. We both ordered the fried chicken and mash potatoes meal, along with a glass of wine.

"Pilar, I want to start off by saying that I am sorry for how everything played out with us. I mean, I know we didn't work out, but I wish that we could be some type of friends. We don't even necessarily have to have sex. I just want you in my life."

"Brandon, your girl, or whatever she is, caused me to lose my job. She got flip at the mouth at Duke's and that's why she got punched in her mouth again."

"Duke fired me by the way. If that makes you happier."

"Your best friend fired you? That's fucked up. That nigga fired you because of us. What's the real issue, here? I wouldn't fire my best friend because of some shit somebody else did."

"Pilar, I have a problem."

"I think we have established that. What else is new?"

"I was fired. I'm only telling you this because you are basically the only person who knows about my addiction. He only found out because I gambled away the building permit money, and they came in to shut the place down. He just fired me and didn't even ask for the money back. He offered to pay for rehab too. He doesn't even know about the fifty thousand that I stole from him. That's good, because I can chill for a bit before I look for another job," I said, lying.

I don't plan on getting a job any time soon. I'm just going to scam and finesse even harder.

"Brandon, you need to go get some help for that addiction, seriously, before someone kills you. If I were you, I would legit be scared for my damn life. If I stole from a mean ass nigga like him, and he don't even ask for the money back, I would be scared. You can't honestly believe that man is going to let you get away scot-free, even though he offered to pay for your rehab. Chile, if he found out about that addiction, it's only a matter of time before he finds out about that fifty thousand dollars. As much as I hate him, please return the money.

People these days do not play about their money."

"Pilar, just chill. He is not going to find out. I covered all my tracks. Anyways, I want to take you on a vacation. You're not working and neither am I. Now, we can spend a whole two weeks together. Anywhere you want to go."

She looked at me like I had two heads on my shoulders.

"Brandon, you are out of your mind. You brought me here to tell me about your addiction and thieving ass ways, but have yet to tell me about your womanizing ways. I wouldn't dare go anywhere with you, with someone's stolen money. You need to do better. If I wasn't done with you, I am definitely done with your ass now. I'm about to go," she spat, and threw her napkin on the table.

I paid the check and followed behind her. She was walking down the road, and I slowly pulled up next to her. I let the window down to holler at her.

"Pilar, are you really about to be this childish? I never thought you would be this person."

She didn't say anything, but she kept her arms folded across her chest and kept walking. I knew that she was cold because at night, Florida gets chilly, especially if you live by the beach.

"Pilar?" I barked her name.

She was legit ignoring me.

"Pilar, we are thirty minutes away from your house. How are you going to get home? There are no buses over this way. You must don't know who lives over here. Nothing but rich white folks," I tried reasoning with her.

I was hoping that she got in the car because Florida is racist as shit. It ain't no telling what some white folks would do if they saw a pretty black girl out here walking by herself. I mean, this is a long ass road with nothing but a house every other mile on one side, and the woods on the other side.

"I'll take my chances. Get help, Brandon," she finally said.

She was literally shivering. I could see it.

"Pilar, get your ass… fuck it," I spat.

I let the window up and sped off. I was going to do a U-turn in about five minutes to go back and pick her up. If I had to put her ass in the trunk, then that's what the fuck I was going to do. I came to a screeching halt when lights came out of nowhere and blinded the fuck out of me. Another car pulled up beside me, and two niggas got out and yanked my door open.

Glad I ain't got shit in here. They can have this car. I'll get another one, I thought to myself.

"You thought it was cool to steal fifty racks from my bro, huh?" the voice said, and placed the steel metal to my head.

I knew that voice. It belonged to Baron.

"Wait… wait… let me explain, please. I have the money. Please."

"Blast that fool. We ain't got all fucking night," Bakari growled.

"Please… please…" I begged. "Call Duke… let me talk to him, please."

My pleas fell on deaf ears as I heard the gun cock.

God please forgive me for all my sins, I prayed to myself, as the gun fired and death engulfed me.

PILAR

$\mathcal{T}$he nerve of that fucking nigga to try and take me on a vacation with money that he stole. It was cold as shit, as I kept trucking up the fucking road. I pulled my phone out my purse, and my damn phone was literally on five percent. If I tried to make a phone call, it was going to go dead, and if I tried to text, it was going to go dead, so I was legit stuck between a rock and a hard place. I was tapping my phone against my head trying to think, something I hated doing, when I heard yelling and crying. I looked up and saw Brandon's car, along with two other cars.

"Blast that fucking fool. We ain't got all night," a deep accented voice yelled.

I knew that accent, but it wasn't that nigga Duke. Duke's voice was much deeper but had the same accent. I wanted to run up and yell, but I am an advocate for minding your own damn business. I'm not trying to get blasted. I stood there and watched the whole exchange. I saw the gun go off, and I knew that Brandon was gone. I was so stunned that I couldn't even scream. They got in their cars and sped towards me. Before I could crouch down, my phone flashed, alerting me that I had a text message. The cars came to a screeching halt. I dove in the woods, and started running as fast as I could. I put my phone in my purse, held it close to me, so I wouldn't get caught in any branches. The branches and shit were cutting the shit out of me, and since it was cold, it hurt ten times more. Like the stupid bitch I am, I was running and looking behind me, and bumped into a guy and fell flat on my ass.

"Boo," he grinned. "Where are you off to?" He pointed the gun in my face.

I just sat there and stared at him. I never thought that this would be the way that I would go out. I closed my eyes and waited for the bullet to pierce me. The gun clicked.

"Kari, wait. I got bro on the phone," the other deep accented voice said.

They all started speaking in their native language, and I couldn't understand a word they were saying. I could definitely tell that the conversation was heated as shit. I was muddy, cold, and probably bloody from the cuts and gashes from the branches I was running through. The guy I knew as Kari, grabbed a handful of my hair, and dragged me back through the fucking woods. He didn't even let get on my feet.

"I guess it's your lucky fucking day, bitch. You better be glad my brother want to see your ass. I would have offed your ass."

It was like he made sure that I hit every fucking stick, hole, and everything else that was in the way. I know I'm going to have scratches every fucking where. Having on this small as dress did not help one bit. I was thankful when we got back to the road. There were no cars or nothing on the road, but Brandon's car was still down there. I guess they were just going to leave his body there. They were ruthless as fuck for that shit, and that is no way for a human being to be treated. My feelings were truly hurt for him.

He popped the trunk, and threw me in there by my hair. I swear I was going to have a fucking plug missing. I was in so much pain that I couldn't even reach for my fucking bag to grab my phone. I didn't even try to kick the trunk because no one would hear me because the music was so loud. I didn't even want to try that shit I be seeing on Lifetime, because I'm sure the other brother was following in his car. What felt like hours later, the car came to a complete stop. Twenty minutes later, the trunk came open, and a light was shined in my face.

"Bro, here this bitch go right here. She a tough bitch too, because this bitch ain't shed a tear yet."

The light was moved out the way, and a face came close to mine, and it was Duke's.

"Pilar?"

I didn't say anything because I didn't know what he was about to do. He scooped me up in his arms, bridal style, and carried me in the house.

"Pilar, say something. Are you okay?" he whispered to me.

He took me up some stairs, and in a bathroom, and started running water in the sink. He sat me on the toilet and kneeled in front of me.

"Where are you hurt? Your body is welted up so bad. I can't help you if you don't let me in."

"Your brothers just murdered a man in cold blood, right before my eyes," I managed to whisper. "They just left him there, in the middle of the fucking road, like he was a fucking animal."

Every time I closed my eyes, I saw that gun going off.

"He was a thief, and he had to be dealt with. That's the end of that."

"What the fuck you doing up here? Why are you catering to this bitch? You know her? It's time to off this bitch." Kari bust in the bathroom door with the gun at his side.

"Bakari, get out, now!" Duke ordered.

"Bakari?" I chuckled. "Your name is Bakari."

"Shut the fuck up, hoe. This bitch probably was helping that nigga rob you blind. Where the fuck my brother money at, hoe?"

"I'm a lot of things, Bakari, but a thief, I'm not."

"Bakari, get the fuck out. I'm not going to tell you again!" Duke yelled, scaring me.

Bakari stomped away from the door, leaving us alone. Duke took a towel out the cabinet and put in under the water. He rung it out, and started wiping the mud off of me.

"I can do it myself. Thank you. I want to go home now."

"I can't let you do that, Pilar. Not right now. Let me get you cleaned up so we can go downstairs and talk."

I snatched the towel from him and started wiping myself off. I was sick of him trying to cater to me like he really gave a damn about me. I know for a fact that he hates me, and the feeling is mutual. I finished wiping myself to the best of my ability. The rest was just going to have to come off in the shower.

"Come on, let's get this shit over with," I spat, and limped past him with him on my heels.

I walked out into the bedroom, and it was so beautiful, but I was too pissed to take in the full beauty of it.

"Lead me to where the fuck I'm supposed to be."

He got in front of me, grabbing my wrist, pulling me down the staircase, and into an office. I was now staring at four people who had similar features. They were all so handsome, except Bakari; his attitude made him so ugly.

"'Bout time, bitch ass nigga," Bakari said. "We finna kill this bitch or what? My adrenaline is pumping, and it's not gon' go down until I know that this bitch is bleeding out the—"

"ENOUGH!" Duke yelled at him.

"Pilar, have a seat, please."

"No, I'd much rather stand."

"Bitch, you do what the fuck my brother tells you to do. Duke, I know you not letting this bitch talk to you this way. What the fuck wrong with you, bruh?" Bakari seethed.

"Bakari, you a pussy. I've had it with you and your disrespectful ass mouth," I spat, rolling my eyes at him. "Duke, if you must know, I'm not going to tell anybody anything. I will keep my mouth shut. I promise you. Just let me leave here, and I will never bother you again."

"Pilar... it's not that easy. How do I know that you're not going to say anything? You know as well as I do that we ain't friends. You hate me, and you can best believe the feelings are mutual."

"First of all," I stepped closer to his desk, feeling myself, and got directly in his face. "I *said* I wasn't going to say anything. Now, let me out this mothafuckin' house. I don't give two fucks about putting you in jail. If the Duval County police is as good as police as people say they are, then they will find their careless asses and put them in jail themselves," I said through gritted teeth.

"I don't think you are in the position to be making demands, Pilar."

We stood there staring at each other.

"Clear the room," Duke ordered.

The boys quietly left out the room, and left us alone.

"Pilar, I own you now. You know that?" he whispered, biting his big ass bottom lip.

"You don't fucking own me."

He stuck his tongue out, and traced my lips with it, basically taking my breath away. I was stuck. His tongue was so warm, and I could feel myself getting wet. I had to regain control in this situation because he was breaking me down.

"Just let me go. I swear…swear to you. I won't say anything. Swan is probably worried. She knows that I was leaving with him, and I told her that if I'm not back to call the police. My phone has been dead for a while now. If you're not going to let me go, let me call her."

"I'm going to let you go, Pilar. Oddly enough, I think I trust that you will keep your mouth closed."

"Let's go."

I followed him to his garage, and we got into this expensive ass car. He never asked me where I lived, but thirty minutes later, he was pulling in front of my place. He killed the engine.

"How did you know where I lived?"

"I know a lot of things. Pilar, please don't make me regret this. All you have to do is keep your mouth closed."

"Sure," I said, and grabbed the door handle, but he grabbed my wrist, stopping me.

"I mean it, Pilar."

"Let me go, Duke."

I got out of the car and walked in the house. He didn't pull off until I had shut the door. I rushed into the shower, and cleansed myself thoroughly before I got in the bed. I legit felt bad about Brandon's fate, but he shouldn't have stolen from that crazy mothafucka. I wished that I could shed a tear for him, but if I didn't shed a tear for my own mama, his ass definitely wasn't going to get one.

DUKE

*W*hen Baron called and told me that they found a bitch who saw the whole thing, I didn't think for one second that it would have been Pilar. I had asked Baron to describe her, and the first thing he said was that she had curly hair. I knew then that it was her, and I immediately told him to bring her to me. Seeing her body bruised and welted up had my feeling some type of way. I wanted to beat the fuck out of Bakari for doing her the way that he did, but I had to remain calm.

After making sure that she was inside her house, I sped back home. As soon as I stepped in the door of my house, my brothers were standing there looking at me.

"I don't even want to know where you took her body. As long as you got rid of that shit. For a minute, I thought that you were bitchin' up over her, bro," Bakari said, trying to dap me up, but I just stared at him.

"I took her body home. I didn't kill her. I believe her when she says that she won't say anything."

"WHAT!" they all yelled in unison.

"Bomani, hook me up with her phone. I want to see if she texted anyone after she went inside the house."

My brothers and I went into my TV room. He hooked the computer up to the projector. I gave him her phone number, and within minutes, his smart ass was able to tap into her phone. He scrolled through her messages, and she hadn't sent any messages, or made any phone calls since I dropped her off. During the time that my brothers took out Brandon, she was receiving a text message from her best friend, Swan.

"Mani, type in my name in her search bar."

"You feeling this girl, bro? You can tell me," Mani whispered to me.

I shook my head, and Bomani eyed me like he knew I was lying. I focused my attention back on the screen, where Mani was typing my name in the search bar. A few messages popped up between her and Swan. Swan was telling her that I was feeling her, and that she was crazy not to see it. Pilar only responded to the messages with a blank face emoji. I can only imagine that she was looking like that in real life.

He clicked through the pictures, and all the pictures that she had taken were the same. It's like she never smiled, and she always had this blank look on her face, but it was beautiful. He went to her very first picture, and it was a picture of her as a toddler. She still looks the same except she has a little more color in her skin. She still had that blank look on her face. I couldn't help but to wonder if she ever smiled. He clicked on her videos, and it was like a porn site.

"Uh-oh, here we fucking go right here. Click that shit, Mani," Baron grinned.

He clicked on the videos, and it was nothing but videos of her and Swan getting fucked by several dudes. He clicked on one, and it was a video of Pilar getting a train ran on her. A dick in her pussy, her ass, and one in her mouth. My heart instantly started breaking. They were treating her like she was a fucking slut. My eyes started to water. This girl didn't even love herself. I could tell that on her face in that video. She didn't even seem to be enjoying it. She even pretended to be nutting. I can spot that fake leg shake shit a mile away.

"Bro, this the bitch you trying to save. This bitch don't even give a fuck about herself. You think she gon' give a fuck about you, enough to not snitch?" Bakari spat.

"Turn it off, Mani," I whispered to him.

"You really wanna save this trick ass bitch, bro?" Kari said.

Before I could stop myself, I flew across the room and had him up against the wall, choking him. The more I heard Pilar's fake moans come from the speakers, the harder I choked him. He was clawing at my hands, but I was hurt.

"Come on, bro. Let him go. He was just playing. Let him go," Baron begged.

I let him go and he fell to the ground trying to catch his breath. I turned and looked at the screen just as all those niggas were bringing themselves to a release on Pilar's beautiful body, like she was a sock. I swiped everything off the desk in anger, breaking everything. I went to my room, jumped in the shower, and as hard as I tried not to cry, I did. This whole time, I'm being a fucking asshole to her, and… fuck. I don't even know how I can even begin to make it up to her.

I got out the shower and got in the bed. I couldn't even sleep because those videos were on my mind like crazy. I tossed and turned like crazy. It was like six in the morning, and I was still trying to go to sleep. I couldn't sleep, so I jumped in my car and went driving around. I don't even know how I ended up in front of Pilar's house, but here I am. I put the blunt out that I was smoking when I opened my car door. As I was approaching the door, a cracker came sneaking out. I yoked his ass up in the collar so fast, and pushed him against the brick wall.

"Are you fucking, Pilar? Huh? Are you fucking her?" I kept asking him, as I pushed his fucking back against the door as hard as I could.

While shaking his head profusely, the door came open, and Swan stepped out in a silk robe.

"What the fuck is going on out here? Why are you hemming him up? Bryan, baby, I am so sorry. This is Pilar's *friend.*"

I instantly felt a sting of embarrassment. I put my hands in my pocket, and let myself in the house. Moments later, Swan came in behind me.

"Um, and how the fuck may I help you? It is after six in the morning, and Pilar is sleeping. Why are you here, and harassing my company?" Swan questioned.

"Um, I need to speak to Pilar."

"She. Is. Sleeping. Come back at a later time," she said, trying to push me out the house.

I moved out of the way of her hands and stared at her.

"Okay, her room is down the hall, on the right. Look, Duke, Pilar is not the typical girl. If you want to fuck, then just say that. Do not try to play with her feelings. I know your type."

"Got cha," I replied, because I didn't want to argue with her.

I crept in her door, and she was laying on top of the covers, naked as the day she was born. She had a lamp on next to her bed, so I could get a very good, clear view of her body. Her body was still welted up, and had several bruises all over it. If you looked at Pilar, you would never think for one second that she does all the things that she does. I pulled a rolling chair from under her desk, and sat in it. I stared at her until I saw her starting to stir.

Ten minutes later, her eyes popped open. She closed them tight again, then popped them open again.

"You're not dreaming, Pilar. We need to talk," I whispered.

She didn't even try to cover herself up. She got up, walked between my legs, and leaned over me. I don't know what she was reaching for, but her nipple was close to my mouth. On instinct, I caught her nipple in my mouth, and sucked on it softly. She let me do it for a few seconds. She moaned softly, and then moved out the way. She slipped on her robe and went and popped down on the bed. I had to close my eyes to regroup my mind, because if not, we would be fucking. I didn't want her to think that I was like them other niggas she is used to fucking with.

"Talk."

"You're not at all concerned about why I'm here? I changed my mind. I'm here to kill you."

Nothing. This girl's face didn't budge. She didn't have not one look of fear on her face, and that was scary as shit to me.

"Okay," she shrugged.

"You're not scared?"

"I'm only scared of God. That's it. If it's my time to go, then it's my time to go, but you're obviously not here to kill me, so what is the real reason?"

"Um… I'm sure the detectives will be here soon. What are you going to tell the detectives?"

"I'm not a child. You don't have to coach me to say anything. I know what I'm going to tell them. You can leave now."

We stood there and stared at each other for a moment. I wanted to ask her so many questions; specifically, how could she do the things that she does with random men. Well, I don't know if they are random or not, but damn. This girl is so beautiful. I was staring at her so hard that I didn't even notice that my hand had involuntarily pushed her hair back behind her ear, and she smacked my hand away.

"You are being extremely weird right now. Stop it. Go back to calling me a bitch, and me calling you a fuckboy. I think we co-exist better that way," she said.

"Pilar, what if I don't want to. We are tied together now, and I think we should have at least form some type of—"

"No, we shouldn't, and no we don't," she said as she smirked.

"Well, I guess I should go."

"You should have never came, but—"

Before she could finish there was a knock on the door. A loud knock. I motioned for her to be quiet. We heard Swan talking to them with an attitude, before she burst into the room and slammed the door.

"Girl, it's some detectives here to see you," she calmly said. "What the fuck happened?" she whispered to her, and then looked at me and rolled her eyes.

She shrugged, and before she turned to leave, I grabbed her by her shoulders.

"Don't fuck me on this, Pilar," I whispered.

"I won't fuck you at all, Duke," she whispered back, and knocked my hands off her shoulders.

She walked out the room and shut the door.

"Look, what the fuck have you gotten her mixed up with? Is she gon' have to go on the run or some shit. She already don't have anybody but me and Charlie. She is fine. Don't come into her life, fuck shit up, and then leave. I mean it, Duke," Swan whispered through gritted teeth.

"Who is Charlie?" I asked her, and my eye started twitching.

"After everything I just said, you only heard me say her friend, Charlie. Charlie is her homeless friend. Don't look like that. I told you, Pilar is different."

I cracked open the door, and we crept down the hallway. I could see Pilar's face, and I'm sure she seen me in her peripherals, but she never even cut her eyes at me. She was sitting in front of two detectives.

"Pilar, do you understand what we just said to you? We found your boyfriend with a gunshot wound to the head. We checked the area, and you two were last seen together at a restaurant," one detective said.

"He was not my boyfriend, but I understand what you said to me. You've said it to me three times. I'm truly sorry that I'm not presenting the emotion that you would like for me to present. I've been through a lot, detective, so emotions for me are non-existent. I'm sorry about his death, though," Pilar said, nonchalantly.

This girl was looking him dead in his eyes. She didn't show an ounce of fear. This girl is really broken.

"Understandable, but you were with him last night? I can see that your body is welted and bruised. Did you guys have a fight? You know it's okay if you shot him. You could get a self-defense plea, but if you don't tell me the truth, then I cannot help you."

"I was with him last night. He begged me to go to dinner with him, and I went. He said some foul ass shit to me so I got up and left him sitting there with the shit face. He tried to get me to get in his car, but I refused several times. He sped off, and left me there…walking."

"That doesn't explain your bruises and welts."

"I didn't speak about my bruises or welts, because how I received them is none of your damn business."

"Ms. Harrison, if you are holding back any information from us, you can and will be arrested," the detective said.

"If you *must* know, I'm heavily into S and M. I am definitely sure that you two don't even know what it means, but it stands for Sadomasochism. That big word that you probably have never heard before, is defined as the giving or receiving of pleasure from acts involving the receipt or infliction of pain or humiliation, hence my welts and bruises. When I'm having sex, I like to be treated like a dirty little slut. By the looks of you two, you wouldn't know anything about that," she said.

Those last couple of words were dripping with so much seductiveness, that I wanted to end this fucking interview now. Those detectives were quiet as a church mouse after she said that shit. There was a very awkward silence following that statement.

"Well, Ms. Harrison, we will be in touch. Here are our cards, if you come up with *anything*… and I do mean *anything* else," the other detective said.

I was getting ready to go give that nigga a piece of my mind, but Swan grabbed me. I knew what that fucking anything meant. I looked at her, and she shook her head telling me no.

"Oh, by the way, who's half a million-dollar car is that outside?"

"My John for the night. I'm a very expensive slut, and with your salary, you definitely could not afford me. Good day, detective," she said, slamming the door.

She put her back against the door and slid to the floor, exposing her goodies. I held my finger to my lips so she wouldn't say anything. I went over to the window, watched as they got in their car, and drove away. I took a scanning device out of my pocket, and scanned over the areas where I knew that they had been. I wanted to make sure they didn't place any bugs in the couch and shit. Some of these detectives are real crafty. Once I was done scanning, I gave her the go ahead to speak.

"So, how was that?" Pilar finally asked me.

"You did fucking great. I never would have imagined that shit coming out of your mouth. I'm very, very impressed. They will be pestering you again. They will follow you around and try to get you to change your story; for that reason, I'm going to have a couple of men to follow you around, just so you don't get any bright ideas."

"I don't need a babysitter Duke. If I wanted to roll over on you, then I would have done it while they were sitting here. You don't scare me. What's the worst that you can do? Kill me, too?" she spat.

"TOO?" Swan yelled. "For God's sake, tell me what the fuck is going on."

We both stared at her and didn't say anything. Pilar looked at me, and then back at Swan.

"The good Duke here, has reckless brothers, who wouldn't understand *tact* if it slapped them in the face, and that is the end of that," Pilar said knowing that Swan would catch on.

"Your bruises? Were you hurt?"

"Nope," she said while shaking her head.

"Okay, good. So, how many brothers you got? Which one is gon' be for me?" Swan asked, twirling her hair around her finger.

"Definitely not the one named Bakari. He is the rudest, by far the stupidest man, and most disrespectful man that I have ever met in my fucking life. They all look like him though." She nodded her head at me.

"Okay, well anyways, Pilar, I'm going to trust that you will keep your mouth closed. So, I won't have anyone to keep their eyes on you."

She rolled her eyes at me and sucked her teeth. I tried to hug her, but she pushed me back. Since she wouldn't give me a hug, I left. When I got in the car to head home, I found myself thinking of Pilar heavily. This girl was making me feel things that I have never felt for no other chick besides Edwina. Pilar is probably going to hate me for this, but I was going to put a detail on her anyway; not because I thought she would talk, but because I didn't want her fucking with nobody else, especially now that Brandon was out of the way.

PILAR

*T*oday was the day of the interview. I finally got a call for the interview as Office Coordinator. I was going to ride with Swan because the interview was at nine and Swan had to be at work at eight.

"So, how are you feeling?" Swan asked me as she weaved in and out of traffic.

"I feel okay. I haven't had a job like this before, so if I get it, it is going to be different. I pray I get it because I'm sick of you almost killing me." I laughed as I held on to the door handle.

I glanced in the rearview mirror, and I noticed that this black car had been following us for miles. I'm not the slowest bitch in the world, but I read a lot of books, and I know when I'm being trailed. This is also the same car that had been sitting a couple of houses down, every time I would go walk on the beach. I prayed it wasn't those fucking detectives, but they would have approached me when I was going and coming from the beach. It's weird.

"Swan, make a left at the next light," I said, as I was still looking at the mirror.

"Bitch, if I make a left right here, I'mma have to go two or three miles out the way, which is going to make me late."

"Bitch, just do it," I ordered.

She did it, and the car made the same left. *Shit!* I thought to myself. Swan made another left, without being prompted, and the car made the same left.

"Bitch, what's going on? Why are you acting like we about to be on a high-speed chase?" Swan questioned. She was getting ready to switch her car into racing mode.

"A black car has been following us and I just hope it's not those detectives. I don't feel like talking to them again."

"Girl, fuck them. If they talk to you again, then tell them the same thing. You smart, but I have a job and don't have time to be playing cops and robbers."

She pulled in her job, and in two minutes, the same car pulled into the parking lot. While walking through the parking lot, I walked by the car as they pulled by us slowly. The tint was so dark that you couldn't even see inside. Sitting in the lobby waiting for my interview, I saw two guys in suits walk in. They didn't say anything but they sat across from me. They eyed me, and I eyed them back. I didn't want this moment to be awkward, so I started to put my headphones in, but I remembered they would be calling me over an intercom to go to the back.

After twenty minutes of waiting, they called me to the back. The interview was nice and smooth. I answered each question with ease, and was actually confident with the way I answered them. After the interview, they told me that they would be in contact with me after the interviews were over, and that would be within two weeks. After leaving out the room, I went and knocked on Swan's office door.

"Just a moment," she said from the other side.

I waited about five minutes, and she finally told me to come in. When I walked in, a man was leaving out and I looked at her. She was grinning and I rolled my eyes.

"You are such a slut."

"I learned from the best." She smirked.

"OKAY!" we said in unison, and high-fived.

"So, the interview went well, and I will know within the next two weeks. I'm going to leave here, but first I need to get out these damn stockings. I think I'm going to go downtown, and see if they got something new in the History and Science Museum."

I slid the stockings from under my skirt. I had on a black pencil skirt, a white blouse, and some black flats. I didn't want to wear heels because I knew I was going to have to take the bus back home.

"Girl, take my car, but make sure you bring your ass back ON TIME. I'm not playing, Pilar. You know how your ass get when you go to them damn museums and shit."

"Okay, Mercy, damn." I laughed.

She threw her keys at my head. She legit hated her first name, and it is so funny. I gave her a hug and left. Coming back through the lobby, the suited guys were gone, which was good. When I got in Swan's car, I let the sunroof back, put on her shades, and cranked the music up. It wasn't every day that I got to drive, so I was going to have the time of my life speeding through these streets. I can't even remember the last time I drove, but I do have my license though.

Downtown Jacksonville is always packed, no matter what time it is. I just so happen to look in the rearview mirror, and I saw the black car again. So, I kept driving while I sang along to Chris Brown and Twista's "Make a Movie". I turned into the police station and parked. I wasn't going in there to talk to nobody, I just wanted that car to go away. I waited inside about ten minutes, and left right back out. As soon as I got back in the car, my phone rang with **Unknown** flashing across the screen.

"Pilar's funeral home, you stab 'em, we grab 'em. How can I be of service to you today?"

"Pilar, what are you doing right now?"

I rolled my eyes at the deep accent that came through my phone.

"Minding my business, what about you?"

"What does minding your business consist of?"

"Um, just…that. Good day," I said and hung up the phone.

I turned the music back up, sky high. I looked in the mirror, and saw that the black was no longer trailing me. That was a good thing. I pulled into the museum parking lot and went inside. I was walking around for hours, just reading all the stories that I have read several times, when I looked up and saw the suited guys again. They were staring dead at me. I speed walked around a corner, then dipped around another corner, and two corners later, I was sneaking up behind them. I grabbed both of my mace cans out my purse, and put them behind my back.

"BOO!" I yelled, scaring them.

As soon as they turned around, I had the cans of mace in their face.

"You wouldn't dare," one of them said.

They had that stupid accent, which let me know who had sent them, but for the sake of entertainment, I was going to toy with them.

"Who sent you? Why are you following me?" I questioned, trying to keep my eyes on both of them.

"We don't answer to you, bitch."

"Oh, really." I smiled. "Answer to this then."

I held my breath and sprayed them both with the mace. They both covered their eyes, and I kicked one of them in the balls and took off running. I felt a bullet whiz by my ear, and I turned around and saw the nigga I didn't kick, shooting a gun with a silencer on it. I ducked and dodged until I was outside, and in Swan's car. By the time I was pulling out the parking lot, they were running next to the car, shooting their damn gun. The glass shattering had me screaming, ducking, and driving at the same time. My dumb ass was literally driving like I was on *Grand Theft Auto: San Andreas.*

When I realized that I was safe, I looked out the rearview mirror and saw the damage. They shot out the back window, and the passenger side back window. There were bullet holes in the dashboard, and in her front window on the passenger side. I didn't want to speed home, so I sped to Duke's. I was driving like a maniac on the way there. I pulled in Brandon's old parking spot, and darted inside. I stomped upstairs to Duke's office with the attitude of a Brahma Bull. See, I have anger issues, and when I'm at level one-hundred, nothing can bring me down but my medications.

"Ma'am, you can't go in there. He's in a—" Frank said coming downstairs.

"FUCK OFF, BITCH!" I yelled at him.

I heard him turn, and start following me.

BOOM!

I kicked Duke's door open. He turned around and stood up, watching me jog over to him.

"WHAT THE—" Duke started, but was interrupted with a fucking smack to the face.

SMACK!

"Wheww, shit, bitch." He fell back in his seat, grabbing his face.

"I'll call you back," he said into the desk phone, and then hung it up.

I smacked that nigga with all of the hundred and thirty pounds in my damn body. I was getting ready to smack him again, but he grabbed my damn wrist and squeezed as hard as he fucking could, but I was too mad to feel anything.

"Bitch, if you hit me again, I swear to fucking God it's gon' take twenty niggas to get me off your fucking ass," he said through gritted teeth.

His left eye was not even twitching right now, that shit was damn near blinking because he was so mad, but you think I gave a damn? I was pissed. I started swinging on his ass with all my might. I know I connected with at least two my punches, before Frank pulled us apart.

"YOU STUPID ASS FUCK BOY! I TOLD YOU I DIDN'T NEED A FUCKING BABYSITTER!" I yelled. "THOSE TWO INCOMPETENT IMBECILES THOUGHT IT WAS OKAY TO…TO HAVE A SHOOTOUT IN A FUCKING MUSEUM. A CHILDREN'S MUSEUM. IT DOESN'T STOP THERE. LET…ME…GO, FRANK. THEY SHOT OUT SWAN'S CAR WINDOW. HER CAR IS RIDDLED WITH BULLETS.

I shook away from Frank, and I started wailing on his ass again. He caught both of my wrists and stood up. He started dangling me in the air by my wrists.

"Frank, you couldn't hold this little bitch. Look at her." He started laughing, and started dancing me around, which further pissed me off.

"IF YOU DON'T TRUST ME, WHY DON'T YOU JUST MOVE ME IN YOUR FUCKING HOUSE, SO YOU CAN WATCH ME TWENTY-FOUR/SEVEN THEN," I yelled in his face, and then hacked up a big glob of spit, and spit in his face.

He threw me to the ground so hard, but I jumped right back up, and ran up to him with my fist raised, but he pulled a gun from his waist, which stopped me in my tracks.

"Yeaaaaaaahhh, you ain't spitting that hot garbage now, are you?" He laughed, cocking his gun. He wiped my spit from his face.

I placed my forehead on his gun, and dared him to shoot me. My chest was heaving rapidly. At this point, I didn't care if he shot me or not. This was the second time that a disrespectful ass black nigga with a stupid ass accent pulled a gun on me, and I'm sick of it.

"Shoot me, fuck boy! Shoot me!" I taunted, pressing my forehead in the barrel of the gun.

My blood pressure was rising rapidly, and if I didn't get my medicine, I was going to pass out.

"What the fuck, Duke? Put the fucking gun down, bro," a voice said from the door.

We looked at the door at the same time, and it was his brothers. I only knew Bakari's name, and he looked excited that I was about to meet my fate. The same two dudes that were following me, came bursting in the room, along with another big man.

"Yeah, shoot that fucking bitch," the one I kicked in the balls spat.

Their eyes were swollen and puffy, so I started pointing and laughing erratically at them. I was at the point of no return. My blood pressure was at stroke level, and I was getting ready to pass out. I remember this feeling from the first time I passed out.

"Pilar, are you okay?" Duke asked, putting his gun away, and moved closer to me.

I shook my head, really fast.

"I need my medica—"

My eyes rolled to the back of my head, and I passed the fuck out.

DUKE

I would be fucking lying if I said that Pilar did not turn me on when her ass came in here all warrior princess like. I wanted to throw her on my desk and beat the fuck out of her pussy. Even as she was lying in my arms, my dick was solid as a fucking rock. She was getting ready to say that she needed her medications before she passed out. I caught her, just as she was getting ready to hit the ground.

"Pilar, baby, wake up! Wake up, baby!" I said smacking her face, and rocking her at the same time.

Her body was burning up, like literally on fire. *Shit, shit, shit!* I thought to myself.

"Boss, we should get her to the hospital," Frank suggested.

"NO!" I yelled at him.

Those doctors at the hospital were going to ask questions that I didn't quite have the answers to. I didn't want them to call the police. She was in a bad state right now, and her ass might get to talking, especially after this huge fight we just had.

"Here, bro." Bomani came in with a bucket of ice and wet towels.

I told him to go get more. I sent all of them, but Bakari didn't budge. He just stood there and stared at me, shaking his head.

I laid her flat on the carpet. I wrapped some of the ice in the wet towels, and put them around her neck. I balled up some of the ice in her hands. I took the rest of the ice and spread it evenly over her body. I took one piece and started rubbing it across her forehead, waiting for them to get back with the ice. Five minutes later, they all rushed back with the ice. They each had two buckets full, which gave me twelve buckets of ice. They poured the buckets of ice on her, and it was like her little ass was in an ice bath. We waited, and like two minutes later, her ass sat up like when the Undertaker rises out of his casket. She inhaled so deeply, like she was getting ready to scream so loud. She wrapped herself in her arms.

"Why…why is it so…so cold?" she asked while shivering.

"Frank, get me a blanket out of that closet," I directed him, but kept my eyes on Pilar.

I stared at her, and at that very moment, I saw a very afraid girl. She looked so innocent, as she kept shaking.

"Pilar, how often do you pass out like this?" I asked, because I was genuinely concerned.

She was starting to shake a lot more now.

"WHERE IS THAT GOT DAMN BLANKET?" I boomed, scaring her.

"Sorry, boss, I'm just not used to seeing…seeing you like… this."

I ignored him, picking Pilar up out the ice. I wrapped the blanket around her, sat in my chair, and started rocking her. I turned towards the window so they couldn't see me. She fell asleep, and she looked so peaceful.

"Clear the room. Goldman, call a repairman to fix the door. Thanks."

I looked at her beautiful face, while she slept in my arms.

"Pilar, I'm here. You are so beautiful. You will never have to do another dirty act, to feel loved. I'm here, baby. Let me fix you, please," I whispered, looking in her face.

I could never say these things to her directly. I don't know why, I just couldn't. The cleaning crew had come in to clean up, and the repair man came in record time to replace the door. I picked Pilar up, and carried her to Brandon's old office, and laid her on the couch. I went downstairs, and found my niggas and my brothers sitting at the bar, having a drink.

"Okay, you two." I used my two fingers and pointed at Romano and Rainey, the brothers who I told to keep an eye on her. "What made you think that it was okay to have a shootout at a children's museum? What possessed you to do that?"

"Boss, she maced us. My eyes still burning from that shit," Romano said.

"Yeah, and kicked me in my balls," Rainey added.

"*Yeah, and kicked me in my balls,*" I mocked his punk ass.

"That doesn't answer my question in no shape, form, or fashion. What if you would have killed a kid? How were you going to explain to your family, the reason you're in jail, in the States?"

"Diplomatic Immunity," Romano said coolly.

"Not for intentional murder, you ass wipe. Look, don't follow her anymore. All I asked you to do was follow her, not scare her," I reiterated the instructions that they were given.

"She went inside the police station," Rainey said.

"BOOM! I told you that bitch didn't give a damn about you. Now we all about to be shipped back to the mothafuckin' mother land, barred from the fucking States," Bakari spat, taking a sip of his drink.

"Shit, probably because you scared her half to death. If you were doing your original job, none of this would have happened today," I said, patting at my swollen lip and eye.

None of those niggas said anything about it, because they know I would wig out on their ass. I would give them the same bruises, but worse.

"Or, you could just ask her yourself because there she goes," Frank said, nodding his head towards the stairway.

I looked at the stairway, and Pilar was coming down the stairs, and headed out back.

"PILAR!" I yelled her name.

She looked at me and then picked up a slight jog. I'm sure she thought that I was going to hurt her. I wondered if she even remembered the episode that she had in my office. I haven't really dealt with anyone who had the issues that she has, which makes her more intriguing.

"Pilar!" I called her name, just as she was getting ready to slam the door of Swan's bullet riddled car.

"Yes," she answered calmly, like she just wasn't ignoring the hell out of me.

"Where are you going? You just passed out in my office, not even an hour ago, and you are trying to leave? You are not in any shape to drive, and plus, you can't drive a bullet filled car around. It might raise a few eyebrows, don't you think?"

"Shit. Swan is going to kill me. She swears that something always happens, when she lets me go places by myself in her car," she said, observing the damage and laughing.

"I'm going to get this fixed. Let's take my car."

She looked over at my car, and then back at me.

"Duke, that car doesn't even have a back seat. We all won't fit in there."

"We'll manage."

She told me where Swan worked, and I knew exactly where it was. The ride over was quiet. Well, I was asking questions, but she wasn't answering them. This girl keeps her private life on lock. It looks like I'm going to have go back and snoop some more. She was just going to have to be mad at me. When Swan walked out the building, I blew the horn. She shook her head and started walking towards my car. As soon as she got in, she went smack off.

"What the fuck you do to my car, Pilar? I know something wrong with my car. You got me riding all uncomfortable in this, this 'only fit for one' car. Every time I let you drive my shit, you do something. Where the fuck you get your license from? The fucking gas station, or out that fake ass meat package your ass be eating. First it was two flat tires, second, it was an accident. I'm almost afraid to ask what happened, since the third time's the charm," Swan snapped.

This girl does not let up. I chuckled to myself when I cut my eyes at Pilar, as I switched gears. She was sitting half on Swan's thigh, and half in the middle. She had her arm resting on her leg, and her head resting in her hand. She looked just like a spoiled kid getting scolded by a parent. She looked half-interested in Swan's ranting, which means she was used to it.

"My meat's not fake. Yours is," Pilar shrugged.

I looked at Pilar, and I laughed so damn hard. Like I literally was laughing uncontrollably. After everything Swan said, that was the only thing Pilar responded to. I had tears in my eyes, because I was laughing so hard. When I looked back at them, they were both staring at me like I was crazy.

"You two always have conversations like this?" I had to know, because it was just toooo hilarious.

"Yep. Pilar really don't be listening to me, fully. She has selective hearing. I swear to God. She just like a nigga. I could speak a whole essay to her, and she's only going to respond to something I said in the middle," Swan said, typing away on her phone.

I looked at Pilar again and she shrugged.

"How often does Pilar pass out?" I asked Swan, since Pilar wasn't talking.

"Pilar, you had an episode? Where are your pills? What happened?" Swan asked a series of questions while rubbing her thigh.

"His stupid friends shot at me. They been following me, and we got into this big fight at the museum, and then they riddled your car with bullets. Your car is trashed. I beat Duke's ass though."

"It's going to get fixed on me," I added before she went off again.

"So, two flat tires, an accident, now a shootout. Got it!" Swan nodded her head.

"Can I smoke this?" Pilar asked, picking up a blunt that I had in my ashtray.

"Where are your medications?" I asked her in a serious tone, as she started to light the blunt.

I snatched it out her hand before she could pull on it, and put it in my mouth.

"Answer me first," I said shaking my head, after she tried to snatch it out my mouth.

"That…in your mouth, is my medication. I haven't had the need to take the medication in a few years, because nobody has gotten under my skin to the point where my anger rises. Well, until Duke came into my life and became a nuisance," she said, snatching it out my mouth and pulling on it.

"Nigga, what the fuck is this weak shit?" she asked laughing, right before she started choking.

"Yeahhh, nigga. Weak shit my mothafuckin' ass. That shit come straight from the ground in Egypt. The best shit that you could ever get in your fuckin' life. Take that shit in. You 'bout to be high in a few minutes, my nigga."

She passed it to Swan and she started choking after the first pull as well. When we pulled into the parking garage, Swan didn't even react as bad as I thought she would. It probably was because I told her that I would pay for it, or that good ass weed had her calmed all the way down. We all got out the car and walked around her car. I saw all the bullet casings and was thankful that Pilar wasn't hurt. The moment I thought that, Swan pulled Pilar into a huge embrace. She started crying, telling Pilar that she didn't know what she would do without her. At this very moment, I stopped lying to myself and embraced the fact that Pilar Harrison is my weakness, and being someone's weakness is never a good thing.

PILAR

After the day I had, this shower felt amazing. I even decided to wash my hair. See, my hair is so irritating and so hard to maintain. I swear I wash my hair every two weeks. Every time I wash it, I make a promise to myself that I break every time. I promise myself that I'm going to wash my hair at least once a week. I used my Shea Moisture's shampoo and conditioner for curly hair, and lathered my hair. I plan to comb it out, or let Swan do it. I'm lazy when it comes to my hair. After I put the conditioner in my hair, I let it sit while I rubbed my Pomegranate scrub all over my body.

After rinsing my hair and my body off, I jumped out the shower. When I walked in my room, I saw Duke going through my dresser.

"May I help you?" I spoke, startling him. "If you want panties, I think Victoria's Secret is having a sale on theirs. I think they are like seven for twenty or so bucks. You don't have to rumble through mine. It's creepy."

He didn't say anything as his eyes traveled my body up, and down. My eyes glanced at the tent that was forming in his silk ass pants. I bit the inside of my cheek, and swallowed lightly. He ran his tongue over his lips before biting his bottom one.

"After you are done being a perv, can you tell me what I can help you with?" I asked him.

I went and grabbed a towel. I started drying off and bent over, making sure to give him a full view of my ass and pussy. He didn't make a move like I expected him to. I put on my robe and sat in the chair, instead of sitting next to him on the bed.

"Pilar, I don't trust you," he calmly stated.

I looked at him and started laughing. I thought that he would be laughing with me, but he wasn't. He was just staring at me.

"You're kidding?"

He shook his head.

"So, what the fuck does that mean? Let me guess, you're here to kill me…again."

"Nope, I'm going to take you up on the offer that you made earlier."

I looked at him with a perplexed look on my face, because I don't remember what offer he is talking about.

"You said, in anger, that I should move you in my home, so I can watch you twenty-four hours a day, and seven days a week. Those are your words, not mine. So, pack a bag or two."

"You are not serious at all, my nigga. I was so mad. I didn't mean that shit."

"So, you say things you don't mean when you're angry. I always thought that people speak the truth when they are angry, or drunk."

"I don't care what angry or drunk people speak. I'm not moving in with you, and that's final." I rolled my eyes, and crossed my hands across my chest.

"Okay, I came over here with the intention of you just packing a couple of bags, and coming with me easily, but now I see that I'm going to have to make you come," he whispered.

"You're going to have to drag me out of here kicking and screaming, Mr. Duke."

He inhaled deeply while rubbing his temples. He got up, went in my closet, and pulled out a suitcase. He just started throwing random shit into it. I watched him with a look of disgust, but I was not going to get mad. I didn't want to have another episode, but if he kept throwing my shit around, then it was going to get ugly.

"Okay, look. I'll do it, damn," I finally said, when he started opening my panty drawer.

"I was hoping you would say that."

I started packing my things slowly. I was hoping that I wasn't going to be at his house long. I put the box of things that I got from Lenora's house in my suitcase as well. I zipped up my suitcase and just stared at him. He grabbed the suitcase, and I followed him out the room.

"Bitch, where y'all goin'?" Swan asked, as she was finishing up her nightly yoga.

"I've been summoned to the great Duke's house. He doesn't trust me, so he says. If anything, I shouldn't trust him."

"Girl, bye! That nigga wanna keep an eye on you so you won't get with nobody else. He ain't slick. I don't know why y'all just won't fuck and get it over with," Swan said while laughing.

Duke laughed, but I didn't see anything funny. I told Swan that I would call her later, and followed Duke to a truck. He put my suitcase in the back, and then opened the door for me. I slid over to the other seat, and he got in behind me. The ride to wherever he lived was quiet as hell.

"Pilar, cheer up. I'm not that hard to live with. I promise. You're barely going to see me," he reassured me.

"If I'm barely going to see you, then why am I moving in with you?" I asked, rolling my eyes.

He didn't answer my question, but looked out the window. Twenty minutes later, we pulled up to a gate. We rode slowly through the gate. There were three houses, but we bypassed those, and went all the way to the end of the road. When we got closer to the end of the road, I saw this huge ass house. I mean I ain't never seen nothing this big ever. I mean you could fit like ten of Lenora's house in this big ass house.

"You like it?" Duke asked me, interrupting me admiring his house. "You were here before. You don't remember?"

"I think I came here by trunk the first time, and when I got in the car with you, I didn't look back."

He shook his head, laughing. When the truck came to a complete stop, Duke got out and opened the door for me. He grabbed my suitcase out the trunk, and we started up the steps.

"You live here by yourself?" I whispered, like I didn't want to ask that question.

"Ummm, yes…no. I really don't know how to answer that question, Pilar."

"You don't know how to answer if there is another body that lives inside of this damn palace? You are even weirder than I thought. Let me try to dumb it down. Do you see someone else when you wake up in the morning?"

"Just Mariah," he said, opening up the door.

"Boy, what is your girlfriend going to say when she sees me? How could you summon me here when—" I was interrupted when I saw a beautiful young lady approach wearing a black and white maid suit, with her hand out.

"Pilar, this is my housekeeper and best friend, Mariah. This is the other body that you were inquiring about," Duke said, laughing.

She looked really young, and was beautiful as shit. I couldn't help but to wonder if they were fucking or not. I know how that best friends shit work. She stared at me, and I stared at her back. We were literally in a trance as we stared at each other.

"Shake her hand, rude ass," Duke said, nudging me.

"Oh, I'm sorry!" I exclaimed, and shook her hand really fast.

"Mr. Duke, I have prepared dinner. I only made enough for two. I didn't know that we were going to have company. Which guest room would you like for me to show her to?"

"I'm good. I probably don't eat what he eats anyway. There is a Popeyes up the road that I can go to. I'll be fine if you just have some snacks."

"Mariah, I don't want to trouble you anymore. She can have my plate, and I'll find something else to eat, and I will show her to where she will be sleeping. You are done for the rest of the night," he said to her.

She curtsied and scurried away. I turned my nose up as high as it could go, and rolled my eyes to the ceiling. I would never in my life curtsy to a nigga. Yuck!

"That's your mothafuckin' problem right there. You got bitches treating your ass like you royalty or some shit, and when you encounter a bitch with just an ounce of common sense, you don't know how to handle it, so you disrespect them. I wish I would curtsy for a nigga," I said.

"You know in some countries, women are supposed to curtsy for men, because women are inferior to men. Where I'm from, your ass wouldn't survive a couple of hours because of that smart-ass mouth."

"Welp, I'm in America, jack. Don't plan on going to those parts of the world. So, there's that."

He smiled at me. This was his first time really smiling at me, and I noticed that he had perfect ass teeth.

"I'm going to show you to where you will be sleeping, and then—"

"Wait a minute, what the fuck you mean inferior? Women are not inferior to men. I don't give a good got damn where you live, jack."

It had just registered within my brain what this black ass nigga said. Inferior. He out his got damn mind. He didn't respond to me, but he kept walking up the stairs towards the room that I was going to be sleeping in. He opened the door, and then blocked me from going in.

"What you mean you not inferior to me? Look at where I live, and where you live. I got two degrees, what you got? You got fired from a gas station, and haven't gotten a job yet. I own multiple businesses, worth millions of dollars, and my every day car is worth more than you will ever see in your lifetime. Tell me again how you're not inferior to me?" he snapped.

"All that education, and you're still dumb as fuck. Move. I don't think I will be eating dinner tonight." I brushed past him into the room.

"Pilar, I—" he started.

Boom!

I slammed the door in his face as hard as I could. I locked the door and got in the bed. I was starving, but I wasn't going back out there to give him any satisfaction. Men like Duke get on my fucking nerves. Well, not just men, but people in general. I hate people who look down on people just because they ain't really got much. That triggered the fuck out of me, because I used to get made fun of because of my clothes. The first time I got made fun of for my clothes, was the very first time I met Swan.

First day of elementary school

"Come on, Pilar. You have to go to school. I don't want to fight with you this morning," Lenora said outside of the door.

I didn't want to go to school because I didn't have any clothes. All my clothes were to small, and Lenora couldn't afford any. Well, she could afford them, if she would stop smoking and drinking so damn much.

169

Cisco told me like three months ago that she was going to bring me some new clothes, but I knew that was a lie. She couldn't tell the truth to save her stupid life. I dragged myself out of bed, and took care of my morning hygiene.

After taking care of myself in the bathroom, I ruffled through the dresser to find the best-looking panties I had. I put them on and they hurt because they were extremely small, and tight in my pocketbook area. I remember the last time I wore panties that were too tight, I had to go to the doctor because it started to hurt when I would pee, and my pee smelled so bad. I had to take some nasty ass medicine for a week that turned my pee orange. Yuck! I shuddered at the thought of it. I didn't want to go through that again, so I took them panties off and threw them away. I would have to go to school with no panties, because I knew all the panties would fit the same.

I looked in the mirror at myself. I had put on some little leggings that had holes in them at the knee. I put on a little collar shirt that Lenora got from the Goodwill last year. It was pretty short, and sat at the top of the leggings. I put on some flats that were almost too small. They had a hole in the bottom of them from being worn so much. I guess I can be thankful since we got running water and I'm clean. I walked out in the living room where Lenora was sitting there drinking and smoking.

"You look nice," she said as she coughed from the smoke.

"Thanks."

"When you get home from school, there will be food here. I know you hungry, since you only ate a little bit of oatmeal last night. I'm going to sit on the porch and watch you walk to the bus stop. Come give me a *hug." She thumbed the ashes on the floor.*

I shrugged. We shared a bowl of oatmeal last night, so yes, I was starving. I know we get food stamps, but she sells them to get cigarettes and alcohol. What little money Lenora do get, she gives it to Cisco. So, I'm just shit out of luck. When I made it to the bus stop, I stood there quietly. There were some kids from my neighborhood there, but I hated them so much. I didn't talk to them at all. They always made fun of me because of the way I look. I can't help that my dad was Swahili, and my mom is beautiful and black. Before I got on the bus, I waved to Lenora, and she waved back. I looked out the back window of the bus and saw a car pull up. I guess we will have groceries when I get home. Every time that car would come and leave, we always go grocery shopping. I'm just glad I'm not there, because I hated having to lay in the bed naked while he played in his private area. He never touched me though, thank God! Whatever Lenora had to do to get money, she did it.

I was standing in the breakfast line, waiting to grab my food, when I heard some snickering behind me. I didn't turn around though, because I just didn't feel like dealing with it.

"Can I have two pizzas?" I whispered to the lunch lady.

"No, you cannot get two. If I give you two, then everybody else will want two. Move along," she spat.

"Girl, you know that's Cisco daughter, and Lenora's granddaughter. She probably ain't ate in two or three days. Give her two," another lunch lady whispered in her ear.

I squinted my eyes at her, but I didn't say anything because I was used to those types of comments now. I didn't want to give her the satisfaction so I just walked away. I found a spot at the back of the cafeteria and ate there alone. While eating, I looked up and noticed the kid from across the tracks approaching me. People who lived across the tracks always thought they were better than us. It was the suburbs over there. His name was Buster. What the hell type of name is Buster?

"Are you eating this? My germs," he said and stuck his finger in the middle of my pizza.

I wanted to cry so bad, but I couldn't. Cisco told me that I needed to be tough in a world like this.

"Buster, leave that girl alone. You know she a crackhead. She need to eat," Yanna said.

She was another girl who lived across the tracks.

"She ugly anyway, Yanna," Buster said to her, and swiped my food off the table.

I didn't say anything, but I just reached down to pick it up, forgetting that I didn't have on any panties.

"Uggghhhh, Pilar ain't got no panties on. Uggghhh. She nasty, just like her mom." Buster pointed and laughed.

"Your pappy wasn't complaining," I shot back.

It was like more people were crowding around, pointing and laughing at me like I was a freak show. They made fun of everything that I had on. They pointed out every hole in my shirt and my leggings, until a dark skin girl came over and started joking on all of them. She had them all on hush mode. Buster acted like he wasn't scared of the girl, and she punched him in his mouth so hard, and she slapped Yanna too. I was smiling on the *inside.*

After that happened, the teachers rushed over to us, pretending like they cared about what was going on. They didn't give a shit about us. Well, a couple of them cared, but majority of them didn't. They didn't even send the girl to the office.

"They won't bother you again. My name is Mercy, but please don't ever call me that. Call me Swan. You need some clothes? Mine might be a little big, but I do have some that were a little small for me. I'll bring them to you tomorrow."

The very next day, Swan did exactly what she said, and that was the day that we became best friends.

Ever since that moment, I have hated people who treat people like they are less than because they don't have as much as the next person. That is one of the reasons why me and Charlie are friends. I need to contact him to let him know that I am okay. I couldn't sleep, so I stared at myself in the mirrored ceiling. *This self-centered bitch. Who the fuck has mirrors all over their walls and ceilings*, I thought to myself.

DUKE

Fuck! Fuck! Fuck! I can't believe my stupid ass said that. Fucking damn it. I shouldn't have said that to her, I thought to myself as I stood outside her door. I wanted to knock on the door and apologize because those words were a little harsh. I left the door with a crazy look on my face. When I approached the kitchen, I saw Mariah standing there eating. She didn't have on her uniform, but instead, a t-shirt and shorts. I never realized how shapely she had become, but then again, I didn't look at her like that because she is my best friend.

"Oh, I thought you had retired to bed, Mr. Duke. Is everything okay? Do you need me to do anything?" She fired off question after question.

"Mariah, did you hear that argument?" I questioned.

She looked at me like she was scared to answer me.

"It's okay. You can answer it. I'm not going to get mad, seriously," I reassured her.

"Yes, I heard the argument, Mr. Duke."

"Okay, so you a woman, right?"

"I would like to think I am." She laughed.

"Yeah, that was a stupid question. Do you think I was wrong for saying what I said to Pilar? I feel bad, and I need a woman's point of view."

"Yes and no, Mr. Duke. You were wrong because women in the states were not raised to be inferior to men. The women I have encountered over here are smart, independent, and successful. These women over here do not need men to survive. So, that is why you were wrong for saying what you said. You weren't wrong because you were raised that women are inferior to men. You guys weren't raised the same way. Both of your worlds are totally different, and that is something that you have to remember if you are going to deal with her."

"Yeah, I guess you're right. Thanks for your advice."

"How long is she going to be here? I plan to go grocery shopping sometime tomorrow. What does she like to eat? What is she allergic to?"

I sat for a moment and thought about those questions that Mariah was asking me. I really didn't know anything about Pilar, but her name, and that she was a freak. I hardly know anything about her, but I'm so into her. It's weird.

"Okkkayy, Mr. Duke. Judging by the weird look on your face, you don't know the answer to those questions. So, I will just ask her when she wakes up in the morning." She laughed and retired to her bedroom.

After my shower, I couldn't sleep, so I decided to do just a little more digging on her. I typed her name in the database, and several alarming things came up. Pilar is twenty-four years old, and she was born in Mississippi. Her mother overdosed when she was fourteen, and her grandmother died from lung cancer when she was eighteen.

There was no mention of her father. I kept reading and learned that she was born addicted to crack, and that she used to cook crack alongside her mother.

"Dear God, woman. No wonder you don't really give a fuck about life," I whispered.

I continued to read, and saw that she got a degree from Jackson State University. She has no student loans because she got a full scholarship. She was in several organizations in college. Wow, after reading all these things about her, I legit felt like an ass for saying all those things I said to her. I had to apologize to her. I closed out the browser and opened my security monitors. I wanted to see if she was sleep.

I clicked on the room that she was in, and zoomed in on her. She had her phone in her face, and she was biting her lip. Her other hand was under the sheet. I switched views on the camera so I could see her phone, because I thought that she may have been Facetiming somebody, but she wasn't. She was watching porn. As I watched her pleasure herself, my dick was starting to rise in my pajamas. I pulled it out and started stroking myself, picturing myself entering Pilar's warm folds.

My creepy ass turned the sound on so I could hear her. She sounded so fucking good. Her moans weren't loud, and they weren't soft. They were just the type of sounds that I would like to hear in my ear. Her moans were getting quicker, and her hands were moving faster. She was getting ready to cum. As she brought herself to a release, so did I. She closed her phone out and set it on the nightstand, and it look like she fell right asleep. I cleaned myself up and followed suit.

The next morning, I made it a top priority to apologize to Pilar for the things that I said to her. I pulled my robe on and went knocked on the door. She didn't answer the door. So, I went in the room and the bed was made. I walked in the closet, and didn't see her suitcase. I started to panic. I walked in the kitchen where Mariah was sitting at the bar reading the newspaper. She was cooking.

"Morning, Mariah, where is Pilar? Did you see her?" I asked her.

"No, I haven't seen her. I went in the room looking for her, and she was gone. Suitcase and all, so I thought you had taken her back to where she came from. Want breakfast?"

"No, thank you. I really just lost my appetite. Put my plate in the microwave. I'll eat it when I come back."

I grabbed the first set of keys off the car rack. I looked at the keys, seeing that they were the keys to my jeep. While I was running to the jeep, I was calling Pilar. She was sending me to the voicemail. The first place I sped to was her and Swan's place. I was beating on the door like a mad man. If she didn't open the door soon, I'm sure they were going to call the police.

"What the fuck is your problem?" Swan asked as she soon as she popped the door open. "You waking me up on this good Saturday morning, messing up my sleep. What the fuck you want? What could you possibly want, since you whisked Pilar away from here last night?"

"Pilar's not here?" I questioned.

"No. She's not. Why? Where is she?" she asked with a look of concern.

"Well…we sorta kinda got into a spat, and…she was gone when I woke up. I just want to apologize to her. She hasn't called you?"

"No, Duke. She has not," she said getting ready to shut the door. "Oh wait, it's Saturday, she's downtown feeding the homeless with Charlie at the Salvation Army."

I thanked Swan and jumped back in my jeep. I headed downtown towards the Salvation Army. When I pulled up, the line was wrapped around the corner with homeless people. I found a parking spot and went inside. It was just as crowded on the inside as it was on the outside. I spotted Pilar in a corner, talking to some nigga. She was twirling her hair and smiling and shit while talking to him. That shit had me tight as fuck. I stood there and watched them for a second, and then a lady got their attention, handing them pans of food. I watched her as she served the homeless people, and she had the biggest smile on her face. I could tell that she was genuinely happy with what she was doing.

Damn, she does smile, I thought to myself.

"Can you move, rich boy?" a homeless person said, brushing by me.

I saw the guy nudge Pilar, and then look at me. She rolled her eyes to the ceiling. She whispered in his ear, and he whispered back in her ear, and they started laughing. My left eye started twitching. Thoughts of killing were running through my mind, and if I didn't get her away from that nigga, it was going to be him. She kissed his cheek, and he kissed her forehead.

I made my way through the crowd, disregarding all the ruckus I was causing because people thought I was cutting the line.

"Pilar, what the fuck is your problem? Bring your ass across that table before I beat your ass in front of all of these mothafuckas in here," I snapped.

"Charlie, this is the great Duke. The narcissistic imbecile, who thinks the sun rises and sets on his black ass. The self-centered bastard who thinks he can talk to anybody how he sees fits, and they just bow down like he is a king. The self-absorbed nincompoop who thinks that because he is a millionaire, has *two degrees,* and his every day car is more money than I will ever see in the world, is superior to me. I think that summed him up correctly," she said nonchalantly, while looking at me.

"Pilar, I get it, damn," I said through gritted teeth.

"Charlie, his skin is probably crawling from being in here. Look at him squirm," she laughed, nudging him.

I bit my lip, because I really wanted to curse her ass out and then drag her ass across the table. I took a deep breath, and did something that I have never did in life: swallowed my pride.

"Pilar, I'm sorry," I whispered loud enough for her to hear me.

"What? I didn't hear you," she said, putting her hand by her ear.

"I said I'm sorry. Now, let's go," I ordered.

"Ehh, I'm not done, and besides, I'm not going anywhere where I don't have a voice, and is treated less than because my resume is not as long as theirs. Now, if you aren't eating, please move. You're holding up the line."

I walked out the building and went sat in the jeep. An hour later, her and that nigga were walking out holding hands. He was pulling her suitcase. I got out and approached them.

"Pilar, come on, for real. You are starting to piss me off," I said, grabbing her arm.

"I know. Your left eye is jumping but it's better to be pissed off than pissed on. At least that's what they say. I haven't been pissed on, yet."

Charlie started laughing and shaking his head. I'm glad this nigga was minding his business because I would hate to have to body his ass.

"Pilar, stop fucking playing. Come on, and that's my last time saying it."

"Duke, I don't know when you are going to realize that you and your empty threats don't fucking scare me. You used to them curtsying ass bitches. You got the right one."

"Just go, Pilar," Charlie urged.

"Empty threats, huh?" I said.

She waved me off and started walking away. I picked her up, and threw her over my shoulder. She didn't even kick and scream like I expected her to. I grabbed her suitcase from Charlie. I walked over to the jeep, threw her down, and strapped her in. I put her suitcase in the back. I was getting ready to pull off into the street when she screamed.

"WAIT!" she shrieked.

"What?" I slammed on the brakes.

"Gimme a hundred dollars."

I opened the console and gave her five twenties, without even asking her why. She jumped out the jeep, and ran to put the money in Charlie's hand. I was getting ready to go off on her ass as soon as she jumped back in the jeep. She put her hand up to stop me before I even got started.

"Think of it as your first good deed of the day."

"What's the deal with you and him?"

"Okkkayyy, Brandon, don't start that shit."

"What the fuck? Who you just call me?"

"I called you Brandon, because he asked the same exact question when I first got in his car. The obsession that he had with Charlie was so weird. He would damn near have a heart attack when he would see me talking to him. He would come all extra early to pick me up from work, so I wouldn't talk to him. Niggas start acting like they care when they think their position is threatened. Nigga was really threatened by a homeless guy."

"Whatever," I said waving her off, but she was right though.

I was a little jealous seeing the way she was interacting with that nigga. That nigga didn't look to homeless to me. I was going to be checking his ass out though. On the way back to my crib, she told me to stop at Walmart because she had to buy some things. I can't even lie, being in here is weird as shit. I haven't been in a grocery store in over a decade.

"Why you standing there looking like awkward? Grab a basket, stupid ass," she said.

I grabbed a basket, and started following her around the store as she put hygiene products in the basket. She was bending over picking out fruit, and I was just staring at her ass. I forgot I still had on my pajamas when I left the house, so my dick was starting to get hard. I distracted myself by looking at my phone. I was looking at Facebook, when I heard Pilar giggle. I looked up, and saw a nigga all in her face. This nigga was giving her flirty looks like he didn't notice me standing three feet away from her.

What the fuck? I thought to myself. I cleared my throat and made my presence known. They both turned and looked at me.

"Nigga, who the fuck you think I am standing right here? You all in my girl face like I won't beat the fuck out of you in this bitch."

"Shit, if this was your girl, then your ass would have been paying attention to this petite ass, instead of being in your fucking phone, my African brother," he said, putting his hands in the praying motion and bowing.

He said that last part in a fake accent and it infuriated me. Nothing pissed me off more than when a mothafucka tried to make fun of my country. My hands were around his neck so fast, he didn't even have time to think.

"Duke! Let him go! What the fuck is wrong with you?" Pilar said grabbing my arm.

I realized that we were in a public place, and I let him drop to the ground. He was struggling to breathe.

"And you bring your tack head ass on before I beat the fuck out of you," I spat and mushed her.

She shopped the rest of the time in silence. Every time I suggested something, she ignored me. We were standing in line completely ignoring each other. She was so cute when she was mad.

"Well, well, well, two of my favorite people. The irony of Mr. Lewis's ex-girlfriend, and ex-boss together, shopping, looking like a happy couple," the voice behind me said. "You moved on rather quickly, don't you think?"

"Detective Dickhead." Pilar waved and smiled. "How are you doing?

"I'm doing just fine, and yourself?"

"I'm fantastic. Have a good day," Pilar said, and then turned and started putting her things on the conveyor belt.

"So, how odd is it that—" Detective Sam started.

"Mr. Duke, do you think we got everything we need for the bar tonight?" Pilar asked me not even looking at him or me.

"Yeah, we did," I responded, not knowing where she was going with this.

"I know you guys had something—" Detective Sam started again.

"Are you here to arrest us? If not, we would like to continue on with our day. You've questioned us both, and you got nothing. It'll be in your best interest to just let…sleeping…dogs…lie," Pilar whispered with a glare that almost scared me.

"Are you threatening me?" he asked.

"Nope, we are just two customers who are having a general

conversation. That's all. Good day, sir," Pilar said as the cashier was telling her the total.

The detective walked away defeated. She pulled her card out and swiped it.

"How did you know he questioned me?" I asked because I didn't remember telling her that those detectives came by the job.

"I didn't. It just felt right to say at the time. It's a good thing that he did, or we would have been up shit creek, huh?" she laughed.

"Ma'am, your card declined," the cashier said, trying to hand it to Pilar.

"Run it again," she ordered.

"I've ran it twice. As debit, and credit. The card doesn't work."

Pilar snatched the card from her and stomped away. I paid for the groceries, grabbed the bags, and walked away. She was standing at the ATM machine, staring at the screen.

"Pilar, I paid for it. It's all good," I said to her. I glanced at the screen, and noticed that her account was in the negative.

"Thank you," she whispered. "I'll pay you back."

The ride back to my place was quiet, and I could tell that her money situation was on her mind heavily. I wanted to get her mind off of it.

"So, why did you say that to the detective back there?"

"Well, he wasn't on the clock, so he can't use that against me or us, if we were to ever get arrested. So, we good."

"How long have you been doing that feed the homeless shit?"

"I started a few months after I moved here. I started doing stuff like that in college. So, tell me about Mr. Duke."

There was a lot to tell about me, but I wasn't sure on how much to tell her. I definitely wasn't telling her about my royalty status, nor my fiancée. A part of me wanted to tell her, but I know the type of woman that Pilar is. She will leave me alone. Well, we not together, so she couldn't be mad. Just to be on the safe side, I wasn't going to tell her. I settled with telling her about me and my brothers moving here for a better life. That wasn't a big lie. Hell, it was halfway the truth. She won't ever have to find out about my whole other life in Egypt, hopefully. I didn't even tell her my real name. She might try to google my ass or some shit. I know I probably won't be able to keep all these secrets for long, but for now, I'm going to roll with it. I smirked as I watched her put on my shades, and lay back in the seat.

PILAR

*W*hen Duke came and got me from the Salvation Army, he turned me on a little bit. If I ever was to get in a serious relationship, it will be with a 'take-charge' man like Duke. I was enjoying the sun that was shining down on me. We pulled up to Duke's gate, and the gate opened. We stopped at the security gate, and the security guy stuck his head out the window. He looked scared as shit.

"Yo, don't let this girl out this gate if you don't hear from me… specifically. You understand me?" Duke ordered.

"Yes, sir," he said.

I rolled my eyes to the ceiling.

"You can't keep me locked in here forever."

"How did you get out this gate anyway? You didn't fuck him, did you?" he asked me, looking at me. He looked at me like he was scared to hear the answer.

"What if I did?" I smirked.

I saw his jaws clench. I bet his left eye was twitching too.

"No, I didn't fuck him. I just told him that I was leaving, and he opened the gate. Who those houses belong to?"

"My brothers."

I nodded my head. Duke's house looked even better when the sun was up. He grabbed the bags, and we went into the house. Mariah had the house smelling so good. When we walked the kitchen, she looked at us like we were crazy.

"Mr. Duke, you went grocery shopping? This is a first," Mariah said giggling.

"Oh, trust, it was like pulling teeth with no anesthesia." I winked at him.

Ten minutes later, she was placing a plate in front of both of us. It looked and smelled soooo good, but I had bought me some food from the deli at Walmart. So, I told her that I would wrap my food up and eat it later. I pulled out my plate, and it had fried chicken, fried okra, and fried cheese sticks. I was tearing it up, and trying to avoid the stares that Duke and Mariah were giving me.

"Okay, I normally don't give a fuck about people staring at me while I eat, but it's just awkward as fuck that you two are just sitting here staring at me."

"How do you fill your body with that ungodly ass shit. All that fried food, and you drinking a soda. Wow! Your pussy probably taste like battery acid."

"It's wild as shit that you know what battery acid tastes like, but the real gag is, you won't ever taste my pussy, so you should be fine."

No matter what I ate, my pussy was gone taste good to whoever ate it. I read a lot of Urban Fiction, and I read about this special recipe in Mary B Morrison's, *If I Can't Have You* book. You whip up a teaspoon of white chocolate extract along with melted pure shea butter, and virgin olive oil. See, I don't like chocolate, so I used peach. I'm a bitch who loves to fuck, so after every shower, I apply my cream. You never know when a dick or pussy appointment was gone drop by. As much as I really didn't like to get my pussy ate, everybody I fucked was intrigued by my pussy, so I ended up lying there getting my pussy ate.

"You sure you don't want this tongue on your pussy?" he asked, and snaked his long, thick tongue out his mouth, touching his chin. His tongue was so big that I'm sure this nigga can lick my whole pussy at the same time.

"Even if I was just the least bit tempted by that thick tongue, I don't like to get my pussy ate, so roll your tongue back in your mouth, unless you a bitch."

They both looked at me like I had two heads on my shoulders. I started laughing because I always get that reaction when I tell people that.

"Girl, you must ain't—" Mariah started.

"Yes, I have. I have several men down here eating this thang, but I just don't get anything out of it, but when a woman is down there… I love it. I don't cum from neither sex giving me head, but I just like the feel of a woman's tongue better. No big deal."

"You don't cum from head? What makes you cum then?" Duke asked softly and stood over me.

I looked at Mariah, and her ass beat it from the kitchen. I didn't want that bitch to leave me alone with him. There ain't no telling what this crazy ass man was about to do to me. My heart started to speed up.

He smelled so good. I looked him up and down. He had on a pair of matching pajama pants and shirt. His shirt was unbuttoned, and I saw his tattooed chest. I cleared my throat of the lump that was forming.

"Are you going to answer me? What makes you cum?"

He was talking just above a whisper, like we weren't the only people in the kitchen. My clit was starting to tingle. I couldn't find the words. I looked into his deep dark eyes, and couldn't help but to bite my lip.

"Um, I have never cum from penetration nor oral. I can only make myself cum, from clit stimulation. My body is different, and I don't know why, but the statistics says—" I started trying to deviate from the conversation, because I now had a puddle of liquid sticking to my thigh, since I didn't have on any panties.

"You mean to tell me, you have been wasting your precious walls on niggas who can't make that pussy cum. Fuck them statistics, every pussy can cum. It just takes the right nigga to bring it out," he said.

I looked down because I never really thought about that shit. I have been with a lot of niggas, and even some at the same time, and I still have not been able to cum. I thought that maybe I have cum before, but just didn't know it. I thought that when you cum, you are supposed to have an overwhelming feeling, but I never got that before.

"Pilar, can I kiss those sexy ass lips?" he whispered huskily. "Please don't tell me no," he said. rubbing his fingers through my curly ass hair. I was happy that his fingers didn't get caught and ruin the moment.

I looked up at him, just as he was wetting his big ass lips with his tongue. Chile, my clit was thumping to the sound of the drums that was in my ear. He lifted my chin with his index finger, and placed his lips on mine. He kissed me so passionately, as our tongues wrestled in each other's mouths. He sucked on my bottom lip so softly. My eyes were closed, and I was moaning faintly. When he pulled back, my eyes were still closed, but it's like I could still feel his lips on mine.

"Imagine if that bottom lip was your clit, Pilar. You know how much milk you would have over my mouth," he said and winked at me.

He went and sat back in his chair and continued to eat, leaving me standing there with my own nasty ass thoughts. I needed to cool off before I turned into a ball of flames right here.

"Pilar, are you really into that S and M shit, though?" he inquired.

"Maybe, but where is the pool around this palace? I know you got one."

"Sure. Give me a moment, and I will show you around. I just realized that I never did that." He wiped his mouth, and stood up.

He called out to Mariah and started speaking his native language. It was so sexy the way that shit rolled off his tongue. I was so intrigued by what he was saying, that I wanted him to keep talking in that language.

"What did you say?" I asked, grinning. "Say something else."

"None of your business, and no. I'm not a robot."

"Well, if you ain't gon' tell me what you said, then don't be speaking that yadda yadda shit around me. I'mma think you talking about me," I sulked, while crossing my arms across my chest. "What you was speaking anyway, Egyptian?"

"I was talking about you, but what I said is not of importance…

yet. Come, let's go to the pool," he reached for my arm. "And Pilar, you don't *speak* Egyptian. I *am* Egyptian, but I *speak* Arabic.

"It's all the same." I shrugged.

He shook his head and laughed. As we were walking throughout the house, I was in complete awe. This house was so beautiful. I could easily see myself living here forever.

"Pilar, can I be truthful with you for a minute? You know I moved you in here is because I want you to myself. The reason I kept Blizz working so much is because I wanted to see you. This is weird, but I loved to see your face red with anger, knowing that you wanted me as bad I wanted you. Blizz never made your face turn red like I do. Your attitude makes me want to fuck that temper right out of you. I have fucked with a lot of women, but you the only one I have let talk to me any kind of way, and…still live. Our first encounter with each other had my dick bricking up. I haven't been able to get you off my mind since that 'you're excused' the first time we bumped into each other."

"You have killed before?" I eyed him.

"That's all you heard?" He cocked his head to the side.

"I'm sorry, Duke, but I tend to block out that touchy feely shit when it comes out of niggas' mouths. I don't be believing shit these niggas say. They say shit to fuck, and after they fuck, they gone like the damn wind. Don't lie to me, Duke, you just want to fuck." I stared at him.

"I am going to fuck you, Pilar, but that's not all I want to do. I want you to trust me. I'll never hurt you, but here is the pool. I'm going to run out for a second. So, have at it."

I didn't even reply, before I got out of all my clothes and jumped in the big ass pool. This mothafucka was filthy rich. How the hell do you get a big ass pool like this on the inside of your house? The water was just right…lukewarm.

"Aye, you know I been living here for years and I ain't never skinny dipped in my own shit. Consider yourself lucky, brat. I'll be back. If you need anything, Mariah will be somewhere around here," he yelled.

He blew me a kiss and winked at me before he left. I would never leave this house. There is so much to do. From the pool, I could see that he had a full gym and a game room. He even had a mini library. That's probably why that mothafucka is so smart. I swam about ten laps before I got out the pool. It's something about swimming that makes your body tired as shit. I went and jumped in the shower, washed and brushed my hair out, and then jumped in the bed. After swimming, it feels like you get the best feeling in the world.

After what felt like hours, I stirred awake to the smell of Vanilla, Lavender, and one of my favorite smells, Sandalwood. When I opened my eyes, I saw the candles throughout the darkened room. I tried to stretch, and I realized that I was tied to the bed post with rope. I looked down and so were my feet. I started to panic, when I realized Duke was sitting in the corner of the room staring at me. This was the one time that I actually regretted going to sleep naked. I mean, I'm lying here, tied to bed posts, in my birthday suit.

"Pilar, you really are a hard sleeper. I carried you from one room to the next, tied you to the bed post, and you never even stirred in your sleep," he said.

"Why do you have me confined to these bed posts like a runaway slave?" I demanded.

"Interesting choice of words, Pilar," he whispered, as he walked over to me.

He tried to put a sleep mask on my face, but I protested by turning my head from side to side.

"Pilar, don't fight me, please," he whispered. "Relax."

I stopped fighting and let him put the mask on my face. He reached behind my head and fumbled with something. He clicked a button and the bed posts started to rise.

"What the fuck is going on, Duke? Oh my God, I'm in the fucking air. Let me down, please," I shrieked.

"Relax, Pilar. I'm right here, baby," he reassured me.

His voice sounded so good and reassuring. Who the hell has shit like this in their house though?

"Pilar, I want you to relax and listen to the sound of my voice. The smells in this room were a combination of Lavender, Vanilla, and Sandalwood, which are aphrodisiacs. Lavender is for me, Sandalwood heightens your sexual response, and Vanilla is the universal scent for happiness and relaxation."

"Duke?"

"Ssshhhh. Only speak when you are spoken to. You understand me?" he groaned in my ear.

"Pilar, I want you to free your mind. Don't think about anything. Everything that is stressing you out, block it out. Can you do that for me?"

I nodded my head. The next thing I felt was some really warm liquid being poured down my stomach, and soon after something really cold. I assumed it was ice.

"Mmmmmm, that feels really good."

"I know, mama."

He rubbed the oil into my skin, and I could feel him blowing on it. His hands felt so good. Just me being in the air and him massaging me had me on cloud fucking nine. I literally couldn't even think of anything else if I tried. He clicked the button and lifted me higher. I haven't done anything like this before in my life. He rubbed his finger up and down my pussy, inserting one and pulling it out. He rubbed his finger under my nose, and then put it in my mouth.

"You like that, mama?"

I nodded, because I was literally speechless. He took an ice cube, rubbing it over my hard nipples. He took the left one in his mouth, sucking so softly. He kissed, sucked, and all but pulled the damn thing off, while he kept the ice cube steady on the other one. The warmth and the coolness were sending my mind into overdrive.

I felt him walk under me to the other side.

"You walked under me, Duke? How high am I in the—"

"Pilar, you're thinking and talking. Don't do either, please," he begged.

He gave the other nipple the same treatment, sending my body into feverish levels. My body was so hot. I jumped a little when he started pushing slightly on the bottom of my stomach. He started kissing between my thighs, and I wish I could push him away. My thighs were so ticklish.

"Pilar, this thang poking out at me. You aight?" He chuckled.

I didn't respond, and didn't even have time to, before I felt him plucking my clit. He started kissing on my juicy center. He licked his long tongue down my pussy, and his tongue covered my whole pussy like I thought it would. Just like he sucked so gently on my bottom lip in his kitchen, he did the identical thing to my clit. It wasn't fast nor slow. It was the perfect pace. He pushed on my mound, while squeezing the bottom of my stomach simultaneously. The pressure… the sensation…I'm getting ready to lose it.

"Let it go, Pilar. Don't think. Let it happen. I feel it, mama," he groaned in my pussy.

I did exactly as he said, and I whimpered loudly, as I felt the fluids squirt out my pussy. My body was shaking, but Duke kept eating. I felt my body getting weak. He finally stopped eating as I felt a second gush of liquids leak out of my body.

"Shit, yeah! You told me that pussy didn't cum, Pilar. You squirted, then you came all over me, girl."

I was still trying to control my breathing, when I heard the button click. He let me legs down, and kept my arms in the air. My body was literally diagonal in the air. I heard the clothes hit the floor. He tapped his dick against my pussy a few times, and then rubbed his whole up my clit so I could feel the length and the girth. My mouth started salivating at how big his dick was. I ain't had a dick that big in my mouth, nor my pussy, but I was gon' take that bitch today.

"Duke, I wanna taste you. Pleeeassseeee," I begged.

"Ssshhh," he quieted me.

He grabbed my hips, positioned the head of his dick at my opening, and pushed himself inside me slowly.

"Shit, Pilar," he whispered, as he pushed all the way inside me.

I could feel the stretching in my walls. This man was touching a spot that I had never touched in my life. He pulled out, and went right back inside me. I was so helpless. I couldn't even run from this big ass dick.

"Dukkke, I can't…can't take this," I moaned.

"Yes, you can," he grunted as he picked up the pace. He started pushing on my mound, and squeezing the bottom of my stomach again.

"Daddddy, oh my fucking…ahhhh," I moaned as my body erupted all over again.

My body was shaking involuntarily. He pulled out, and a couple of seconds later, he pulled the mask off my face. We were staring into each other's eyes before he pressed his lips on mine.

"Look at yourself," he whispered.

I looked at the ceiling, and I chuckled at the way I was hanging in the air. He had a mirror on the ceiling and on the walls, just like the other room. He positioned himself back in between my legs, and went back inside me. It's one thing feeling it, but actually seeing it had me feeling so fucking good. I watched the mirrors as he went in circles inside my pussy, making me have another orgasm.

"Ahhh, shit! Mama didn't need my help this time. Lemme find out." He smirked.

He let the bed posts back down, and as exhilarating as it was being in the air, I was happy to be out that mothafucka. This crazy shit is an 'only on anniversaries' type shit. He untied me and threw the ropes on the ground. He stood up beside the bed, stroking his dick. I needed him in my mouth.

"Slide over here. Stay on your back," he ordered.

He grabbed my hair, yanking my head back, and tapping his dick against my lips. I opened my mouth, and he slid his dick in my mouth. He fucked my faced, and tapped my hand every time I tried to touch his dick. He pushed his dick in my throat, and it still wasn't all the way in my mouth.

"You like this shit, don't you?"

I nodded my head.

"I need to get back in that pussy, Pilar. Fuck!"

He pushed me up against the headboard. He put my legs on his shoulders making my knees damn near hit me in my face. I'm glad I'm flexible. Shit! He put his dick in me, and started fucking me like his life depended on it. He intertwined our fingers and put our hands up against the wall, as he continued to fuck me.

"Dadddyyy, oh my fucking God. Daddy, please... you're tooooo deeeppp," I moaned.

"No...no such...thing as too deep," he grunted.

I laid my head back against the headboard. I looked to the right and got a glimpse of our bodies meshed together. The feelings became overwhelming as he pounded into my swollen pussy, and the tears started falling down my face. I don't even know where they came from.

"Duke, babyyyy, you feel…you feel…so good," I sniffed. "Please don't hurt me."

He slowed completely down to just long deep strokes. He let my hands go, pulling my chin up towards him.

"Open your eyes and look at me," he demanded.

"Don't cry, baby. I will never fucking hurt you. You're too beautiful, baby. Damn, you gon' make a nigga fall in love, Pilar. Fuck! I'm halfway there, Pilar. Please look at me. I'm feeling you, baby. Don't you hurt me, shit! I'm yours, and you're mine. I swear to fucking God. Pilar."

I searched his eyes to see if I could tell if he was lying or not. His eyes told me that he was telling the truth. His eyes were starting to water. It's like we were looking into each other's soul. He rubbed his hand up and down my face, and placed his lips on mine, making love to my mouth.

"Pilar, I don't want anybody but you. I swear to God. Cum with me, Pilar. I can't hold this shit no more," he whimpered against my lips.

He rocked inside me one more time, and on cue, my body erupted for him. We sat there in that position for a few minutes and just stared at each other.

"Pilar, I'll kill you for real. On my life. Don't fuck with another nigga, ever again. Dead all that shit. You understand me?"

I guess I didn't answer him fast enough. He grabbed my neck, pushing my head into the headboard.

"I asked you did you understand me?" he spat through gritted teeth, squeezing my neck just a little tighter.

At the same time, my pussy muscles clamped down on his dick. Choking doesn't bother me. I love being choked. He raised an eyebrow and looked down. He squeezed my neck harder, and then he pushed on my mound, and I felt my body shudder.

"That pussy just spit on my dick. I knew you liked that rough shit. You think another nigga can make your pussy do this?"

I shook my head.

"Did I make myself clear? No fucking nobody else. It's just me and you."

"I…I understand," I whispered.

After we got out the shower, he carried me back to the other room, because I could barely walk. As soon as my head hit his chest, I was out like a light.

DUKE

*W*hen I stirred awake, Pilar was still laying on my chest. This skin to skin contact made me get butterflies and shit in my stomach like a bitch. Laying here looking at Pilar sleep has to be one of the top moments in my life, ever. I rubbed my nose through her hair, and it smelled amazing. She told me that she washed it after she got all the chlorine in it, and now it smelled like peaches. Last night was on my mind so fucking heavy. Everything I said to Pilar last night was the truth. I only wanted her, and I probably would hurt her if she ever fucks or talk to another nigga. My mind went to Edwina. The girl that I'm supposed to marry. The girl who has been with me since I was sixteen years old, and to my knowledge has never fucked around on me. Hell, she's carrying my child. I don't even know what the fuck I'm going to do. Eventually, I'm going to have to go home and get married. Where is that going to leave me and Pilar? Maybe I can convince her to be one of my wives, but I promised Edwina that I only wanted one wife, so I'm still stuck between a rock and a hard place.

I grabbed the remote and opened the curtains a little bit, to let some of the sunshine through. When I got up to empty my bladder, Pilar stirred, but turned on her stomach and went back to sleep. I slid back in the bed next to her, and started rubbing on her ass. I placed soft kisses down her back to the top of her ass.

"Hmmm, baby. Good morning," she moaned.

"Good morning it is," I whispered back.

I bit her on both of her ass cheeks, and then ran my tongue down the crack of her ass. Her moans were so low and soft. I spread both of her cheeks, and swirled my tongue around her asshole. I looked up to see her clenching the sheets. Pilar started poking her ass out, giving me more access to suck on those pussy lips. I sucked on those fat ass pink lips like it was freeze pop on a hot day.

"Mmmmm, daddddddyyyyy, I'm finnaaaa cummmm," she moaned.

I caught every drop of her cum. My dick was standing up, ready. I spread her ass cheeks, because I wanted my first stroke to be deep. I watched her pussy coat my dick with her cream, while she moaned and threw it back on me, slowly.

"Ohhhh myyy goodness, daddy. Pleaseeeee, just the tiipp," she moaned, trying to push me back.

"Hell naw, Pilar. You can't see what I see, boo. Shit!"

She kept trying to push me, so I grabbed her wrists and pushed deep as I could in her. She clamped her muscles down on me, and made me shoot off in her earlier than expected. I caught my breath, and let my soft dick fall out of her.

"Pilar, are you on birth control?" I whispered, still trying to catch my breath.

"No, you're the first guy I ever let hit without a condom. I'll go get on something, if you want."

"Hell yeah, because after hitting this good shit with no rubber, ain't no way I'll put on one now." I laughed, smacking her on her ass.

"Mariah should have breakfast ready. You can come out whenever you get ready," I said, kissing her forehead.

"I'm just going to lay here for a little while." She smiled.

She turned over and hugged the pillow. I bit my bottom lip because that girl just turns me on doing the slightest shit. I put my pajama pants on and went into the kitchen. Mariah was putting the plates on the breakfast in bed tray.

"Good Morning, Mr. Duke. I thought I would be feeding you two in bed this morning. Did it work? Did she…you know?" Mariah asked excitingly.

Mariah was referring to her idea that she gave me. She told me that I needed to make sure that she was really relaxed, and her body would do whatever it was that I wanted it to do. She had me researching different type of smells and shit that would set the mood. I tied her up on my own though. I don't even know why I had that lifter installed, because it's not like I brought a girl here, but since Bomani created it, I had to test it out. Pilar was the absolute perfect person for it. I bit my lip as I thought about how many times she came for me.

"How many times, is the question. She felt so fucking good to me. The way her body responded to me. It was like…perfect. Mariah, this is not going to be good. I need her. I want her. But—"

"Edwina?" She smacked her lips.

I nodded my head.

"Mr. Duke, you know this is only going to get worse. There will be no winner in this. You stay with Pilar, you know the King is not going to go for that. You cannot be King and marry somebody outside of Egypt. It's funny that you can have as many wives as you want, but if you marry someone outside of Egypt, you'll damn near be banished from the country. You have a lot on your plate, Mr. Duke," she said, shaking her head.

"Another thing. She's pregnant."

"Wow! When did that trick get pregnant?" Mariah rolled her eyes, sipping her coffee.

See, Mariah and Edwina cannot stand each other. First, because Mariah and I have been friends since forever. At first my mom thought that I would marry her, but we were just best friends, that's all. The only woman female friend that I have. She also didn't like Mariah because I let her come over here and work for me, instead of her. Third, because women over there are just like women over here—don't like each other for the fuck of it. You should see how they act when they get around each other. They be trying to pretend to like each other, and it's so funny.

"You know what, Mariah, that is a very good damn question. I went over there, and she was like eight damn weeks. I'm trying to calculate in my head and shit, but I don't want to think about her cheating on me."

"If she did, would you be mad? You know your ass ain't been faithful since…hell, have you ever?" Mariah laughed.

"Hol' up, don't play me. I have been faithful. My dad said she don't even go nowhere, except when she goes with my mothers. So, I don't know. You know y'all women crafty as hell. If y'all wanna cheat, y'all mothafuckas gon' find a way to cheat." I laughed.

"What's her story? She seems like a very sweet girl, but has something internal going on."

"Mariah, she had a troubled childhood, but that's only what I read. I haven't heard from her mouth specifically, but I know that she is broken, mentally and emotionally."

Mariah instantly started shaking her head.

"Duke, you can't do this to her. If she is *broken* like you say she is, then you have to tell her. You have to tell her that you cannot be serious with her because of the position that you in. If she wants to stay after you tell her, then that's on her, but you owe it to her."

I knew that Mariah was serious because after I stopped her from calling me Your Majesty, she called me Mr. Duke, but when she is serious she calls me Duke. I stared at her as she continued.

"I am a woman, I know how it feels to be broken time after time by a guy. Trust me. Since I been living over here, I have had my heart broke several times, to the point where I just stopped trying. I mean, I would rather date those men back home, at least I know they are going to fuck with other women and not lie about it. Trust me, Duke. Do the right thing. If you don't, it'll bite you in the ass in the long run. Hell, your ass might end up getting hurt instead of her."

Before I could respond to her, Bomani and Baron walked in the door sniffing like some damn dogs. They started eating off the untouched plates that were on the breakfast tray.

"Good morning, Prince Duke," they said and bowed.

I laughed at them. I legit hated when they did that, outside of when they are supposed to do it. They only do it to fuck with me. I honestly just wanted the respect. They didn't have to do all that shit they do when my dad is around.

"Where is my middle brother?" I asked.

"He might be on his way back from Egypt. He been over there for about a week now. Nigga, where the fuck you been?" Baron said.

"Nah, bruh. I ain't know. He ain't told me nothing, but it's cool though. How was Miami, and New Orleans?"

I sent my brothers to check on my other businesses, since it's been a while since I showed my face. I did speak to my general managers every day though. I also hired something like a secret shopper to drop in every other day, to make sure everything is running smoothly.

"They were straight. Lines were still around the corner, but I was also thinking about you getting a bigger place for New Orleans though. That bitch was jumping, and you legit had to wait for some people to leave to let some people in, because you didn't want that bitch to get shut down. You know them pigs be waiting for one thing to go wrong, but because you are my brother and I love you, I took the liberty of finding you a bigger—" he stopped. "Well, hello. This is a nice surprise." Baron smirked with his eyebrow raised, looking past me.

I turned around and saw Pilar standing at the opening of the door, rubbing her eyes, childlike. She had on my silk pajama top, and it damn near swallowed her. She waved at my brothers. Mariah smacked

Bomani's hand from Pilar's plate.

"I know you are hungry, and you should eat something. Come, sit," Mariah ordered.

As she walked past me, I grabbed her, pulling her between my legs. I cupped her ass and pulled her even closer to me. I wanted her to feel this dick getting hard for her little ass.

"You sleep good?" I whispered against her soft lips.

"Yes, daddy," she replied, grabbing my ears.

Once she bit my bottom lip, it was over. We were kissing so passionately. I sucked on her tongue softly, and listened to her low moans. I ran my hands under the shirt, and had a handful of her ass. I could feel that pussy getting wet. I slipped a finger inside of her inviting pussy, and started fingering in. Someone cleared their throat.

"If I wanted to watch amateur porn, I would log into Pornhub," Baron said as he laughed.

I pulled back and stared at Pilar, whose face was bloodshot red. She was embarrassed, but I wasn't. That kiss made me forget that I was even in the kitchen with my brothers and Mariah. Yeah, I realized that Mariah was right; if I don't tell her soon, this was going to end bad. She sat down and started to eat. The more I watched her, the more I wished that I wasn't in the predicament that I was in.

"Stop staring at her, creepy ass nigga," Baron said in our language. "What is going on here?"

"A horrible situation. Horrible, horrible situation, that nobody is going to win in," I replied in our language.

"I told him that he has to tell her, or someone is going to end up hurt," Mariah chimed in.

"Bro, you really feeling this chick, and you know you can't take her home. You can't marry her. You can't do shit with her, but show her a good time. You guys have no future together. Cut it off before you kill her," Bomani added.

I watched Pilar as she watched our exchange. I could tell that she was getting ready to get upset because she couldn't understand what we were saying.

"Why would I kill her?" I asked, stroking my beard.

"You love her. The way you look at her. The way that she talks to you, disrespects you, and you let her live. You love her, and you're not supposed to, Barak. You will kill her before you let another nigga have her. You know I'm not lying," Bomani said.

"That's true. All of it. I love her, and I will kill her if she even think she gon' give another nigga that pussy."

"Hol' the fuck up. Don't be—" Pilar started.

"End it, and soon. Your birthday is approaching quickly," Baron said quickly.

"Look, like I told Duke and Mariah earlier, don't be speaking that yadda yadda shit around me because I can't even understand what the fuck y'all be saying. Y'all could be talking about me, especially if y'all can't say the shit in English. All y'all got me fucked up, if we being real."

"Calm down, pretty girl. It's a habit," Baron laughed.

She rolled her eyes at him and took her last bite of food. She got up and washed her plate. She stomped back to the room, and I heard the door slam.

"Well, you go take care of that and I will holla at you later." Bomani laughed.

They left out the house, leaving Mariah and I in the kitchen together. She patted me on the back and left out the kitchen. Instead of going in the room where Pilar was, I went and sat on the balcony. I couldn't help but think about the ending of this shit. I really needed this shit to work, because I don't want to lose Pilar, and I don't want to lose Edwina, nor my crown. When I move back home, Pilar can't come with me. I wonder will she be cool with seeing me once a month, if that? As King, I'll barely have enough time to travel here. I rubbed my temples.

"What's going on, Duke?" Pilar asked, as she came through the sliding door. "You look stressed."

"Nah, I'm good, mama. Just out here looking at the scenery, that's all. Come sit," I patted my lap.

She straddled me. As we were gazing into each other's eyes, I realized that I have feelings for somebody that I don't even know. Her green eyes are so hypnotizing and filled with pain.

"Pilar, why are you so closed off? Tell me about you. Tell me everything. I have feelings for someone I don't even know."

"I don't normally talk about myself, but what is it that you want to know? Ask me questions."

"Start somewhere...anywhere."

"Um, I really don't know where to start. My name is Pilar Harrison, and I'm twenty-four. I'm from a small, small city in Mississippi. The population of people there can fit inside this palace. My mother was a crackhead, who overdosed. My grandmother was an alcoholic, who smoked herself to death. I have a degree in Health Science, and I am still looking for a job. Swan has been my best friend since forever, and my only best friend. Well, when I moved here, I met Lee and Charlie. I like long walks on the beach, museums, and art. I really, really love art. I like to read and do things that no one else thinks about doing. I think that's the gist of my life. Anything else?" She shrugged.

I knew about all that shit. You can google that shit. I wanted her to go deeper in her life. I guess I'm just going to have to keep it a buck with her, and tell her that I saw all that shit in her phone. I still can't get some of the shit I seen out my mind. I took a deep breath because I didn't know how this conversation was about to go.

"Pilar, why don't you love yourself?"

"Excuse me? I do love myself," she said, cocking her head to the side.

"Pilar, if I tell you this, promise me that you will not get mad at me."

She shrugged.

"After I had taken you home that first time, I had Mani to hack your phone. I saw…no, don't get up, please, just hear me out. I wanted to see if you had been texting anyone at the time of the…you know, and I just so happened to see those videos of you. Pilar, you have had multiple trains ran on you. Women who love themselves don't do that."

"You *just* so happened to see those videos, or you went into my videos and strolled through them? You had no right to do that, Duke. I haven't done anything that I'm ashamed of. Is that what your brothers were in their saying, huh? Were they asking you how can you let a hooker, or a hoe, be in here? Were they asking you—"

I hushed her by holding my finger up to her lips. They were quivering. Her jaws were clenching and she was blinking back her tears.

"Pilar, tell me why you don't love yourself. It's okay to cry. When was the last time you cried?"

"I was about six years old. This boy pushed me down and made me cut my back. Cisco, the woman who pushed me out, told me that you are never supposed to let someone see that you are weak. Crying equals weak. The irony of that coming from a drug addict. Before you ask, I didn't cry at her funeral, nor Lenora's, my grandmother. I blocked everything out."

"Continue, please."

She stood up and walked over to the banister. She grabbed onto it, and held her head down. She took a deep breath.

"Can you imagine at six, seven, and eight years old, laying in the bed naked, while a man played with his dick?" Her voice quivered.

"Pilar, I'm sorry, we can do this another time," I pleaded.

She turned, looked at me, and her face was as red as a tomato. The last thing I wanted to do was upset her.

"No, you want to know about my personal life, then let's do it.

Imagine being so hungry that you would do anything for food…for money. I was never touched, but it doesn't take away the pain I felt inside, watching my grandmother…watch an old man play with his fucking dick just to get money. Do you know how many meals I missed or had to share with Lenora, because she wanted to smoke, drink, or give the money to Cisco to SUCK ON A GLASS DICK? Do you know how many kids picked on me because I didn't have any panties to wear to school? They were all tight. Could I tell the teacher? No! Lenora reiterated what happened in that house, stayed in that house, if I didn't want to be sent somewhere, where they would do much worse things to me. At seven, I cooked and cut crack and measured out cocaine for Cisco. I can be partially responsible for my mom's habit, because I fed it to her. Imagine that." She chuckled to keep from crying.

"Pilar, your father. Where was he? He didn't come—"

"FUCK THAT MAN, DUKE! I'm twenty-four years old, and I can count on one hand how many times I've seen that nigga. He knew what the fuck I was doing for money, because Mount Olive is only but so big. He can act like I don't know about his status in the streets, but I do. Did he step forward and say 'here is a few dollars, Pilar? You don't have to do that, Pilar.' Even a simple 'I love you, Pilar' would have sufficed. I have never, ever been told that, except from Swan. She tells me she loves me all the time. I have fucked his friends for God's sake, and he never so much as sent a text, telling me how ashamed he was of me. I would have rather him said that, than nothing at all. Can you imagine your daughter fucking your friends just to get an ounce of attention from you? It's alllll one big cycle for the Richardson girls. Cisco fucked for her drug money, Lenora fucked for her ciggs and alcohol, and precious ol' Pilar fucked to have a meal. The nerve of that man to be standing on Cisco's grave telling me how much he loved her, and that I wouldn't understand. If I had a gun, I would have shot him dead. He had his little snooty ass family across town who thought he could do no wrong. I never met my grandmother or my grandfather on his side. They swear that my mom was a whore who trapped him, and I'm probably not his. I'm the spitting image of him, hell."

"Pilar... I'm sor—" I started, but she held her hand up, stopping me. The tears were flowing so freely down her face. She needed this. This has been crammed into her little heart.

"Don't be sorry...don't feel sorry for me. I am good. I'm not ashamed about anything I have done. You asked me why I don't love myself; oh, but I do. I love myself more than anything in this world, Duke, and that's why I did what I did. I knew I wouldn't be doing that forever. So, now that you know everything, you can go and tell your brothers that this hoe will be leaving your hair. Do what you will with the newfound information. I'm gone," she offered me a weak smile, but the tears were still coming down her face.

I tried to grab her hand as she went back through the sliding door, but she snatched away. I couldn't help but to cry for her. I felt so bad for her. There is no way that I could have a daughter out here and let her do the shit she did. Hell, I would kill every one of my fucking friends if they looked at my daughter, let alone fucking touched her. I had to let her know that I was here for her.

I rushed through the glass door, and saw Mariah standing there wiping her eyes. I guess she heard the whole thing, but I didn't have time to say anything to her. I ran downstairs just as Pilar was walking through the front door. I ran behind her, and grabbed her hard as I could without hurting her.

"Pilar, baby, I'm here for you. Pilar, I love you," I whispered in her ear. "Look at me."

She turned around and gazed into my tear-stained face.

"Pilar, I love you. I fucking mean it. You'll never have to do any of that god forsaken shit again. I love you. I promise I'll show you every fucking day how much. You won't even think about that nigga not telling you that shit. Please, let me apologize for how things went in your life. Pilar, you are mine now. You my woman, and I'm your man. I don't give a fuck about that shit. You understand me?"

She nodded her head. I picked her up, wrapping her legs around my waist, and carried her upstairs. We made love on and off for the rest of the day. I don't know what's going to come from this, but I knew at this point I was deeply in love with this woman, and it ain't a damn thing nobody was going to say about it.

PILAR

*T*hese last few months have been nothing short of amazing. Duke has kept his promise, and has showed me nothing but love since that day in his foyer. Believe it or not, I haven't even told him that I loved him, but I'm sure he knew that I did. He showed me, and I showed him. Since I've been living with him, Mariah and I have become best friends. Hell, Swan accepted Mariah, and now Lee, which made me very happy. I thought those two would never become friends. Things were finally looking up for me. His brothers were very much supportive, except Bakari. Well, I don't think that he knew, because we always missed each other. When he would come over, I would be gone or sleep. So, we always missed each other, but I'm not in a rush to let him know that I'm with his brother.

Duke told me that I didn't have to work, but I wanted to. I needed to earn my keep. After much begging and dick sucking, he told me that I could work at the pool hall. I was going to walk around and serve drinks. Me and my girls were in the mall looking for me a sexy outfit to wear.

"Bitch, look at this. I need this for myself," Swan said, holding up a black corset outfit to her chest.

"Lari, what the hell you want to wear? You know you damn near got to wear a nun suit. Duke ain't gon' be feeling you wearing your titties and ass out. You better pick one," Lee said.

"You sho' ain't lying. You better be glad he didn't see what you had on before you left today, or he would have been heated. That man don't want nobody looking at your sexy ass, and I don't blame him. Your ass has gained so much healthy relationship weight. That weight got your ass thick in all the right fucking places." Mariah laughed while groping my ass, making it jiggle.

I can admit, I have picked up some weight since I've been with Duke. At first I thought I was pregnant, but I wasn't. He told me that I didn't have to get on birth control, and I was happy about that, especially with all the side effects that they have now.

"Alright, Mariah, you acting like I won't have your ass eating this pussy. Don't you forget I like women too," I warned her.

"Whatever. You know I don't go that way," she stated as she laughed.

"Yeah, that's what they said too, but anyways, I found it. This is the outfit for my debut night as a drink server."

I had a black leather thong corset outfit with some fishnet stockings. I even purchased some thigh high red bottom boots. A bitch was going to be bad tonight. I wasn't going to go back to the house because I wanted to surprise Duke. As soon as we made it to Swan's place, she immediately started on my hair. See, it literally takes three hours to get my hair bone straight. I chose to get it straightened because Duke always asks me how long is it. He was going to see tonight. My phone alerted me that I had a text message.

Duke: *1 image attached* *Damn, Ma! Where you at? I need those warm ass lips on my hard ass dick right now. You see my shit.*

"Damn, bitch! I see why you sprung as hell on that dick. That shit can barely fit in the whole damn picture. I wonder if one of his brothers are hung like that, because shit, that—" Swan started.

"First of all, bitch, can we not keep talking about my nigga's dick? Focus on my hair, shit. I don't inquire about his brother's dicks, so I don't know. They wasn't lying when they said those foreign niggas will fuck up your life. Babyyyyyy."

Me: *You are tooo fucking spoiled Duke Ramses. I'mma suck your dick tonight, like I always do.*

Duke: *If only you knew how much I am whining right now. I know I'm spoiled. Didn't nobody tell yo beautiful ass to come in my life, and suck my dick morning, noon, and night. Shit! A nigga get used to shit like that. I guess I'll see you tonight. Love you, ma! Be safe.*

I didn't reply, but he texted again.

Duke: *Y'all ain't driving either. I'll have Romano, and Rainey to come pick you guys up.*

Me: *Okay, baby.*

When Swan finished my hair, I admired myself in the mirror. She gave me a middle part, and my hair flowed down to the top of my ass. Swan wrapped it up for me, and I got in the shower. We were just finishing up when we heard the horn blow outside. I admired myself in the mirror. Swan also beat my face to the capacity. I literally looked like a high-priced hooker with all this cleavage and ass out.

"Y'all, they out… GOT DAMN, PILAR! Duke gon' fuck the shit out of you in his office. I can feel that shit right now," Mariah said.

"Nah, bitch, wait until I comb this hair down," Swan said.

I sat down and let her comb my hair down. Mariah and Lee looked at me like I was crazy.

"Lari, bitch, you are sexy as fuck. Why you don't straighten your hair often?" Lee asked, rubbing her fingers through my silk wrap.

"She a lazy ass bitch, and would rather me stand on my feet for three hours," Swan answered.

I rolled my eyes at her response. We went out to the truck, and as soon as we got in, they started talking shit.

"Damn, what the hell y'all had to do. We been waiting out here for twenty minutes," Romano spat.

Mariah yelled at him in their language, and whatever she yelled made him turn around and shut the fuck up. On the way to Duke's, we had a couple of shots. They was ready to kick it, and I was ready to have fun. They dropped us off in the parking garage. I saw that Brandon's name had been replaced with Goldman's name. I walked behind the bar like the boss bitch that I am, ignoring all the dirty stares and eye rolling I was getting.

"Frank, where you want me to start?" I asked.

He was turned towards the counter and didn't see me. When he did turn around, he squinted for a few seconds and then smirked.

"Pilar? Girl, you gon' get it. You know that right?"

"I ain't worried about Duke, chile. Just give me this damn tray."

He handed me the tray and told me that I was going to work the right side. As I was walking down the aisles, all the niggas were stopping and getting drinks. They were also putting hefty tips in my corset. I was excited. I hadn't made any money on my own in a long time. I spotted Duke, Baron, and Bomani, standing by a machine, talking. I didn't want them to notice me, so I tried to slide by. I thought it would be easy since Duke's back was to me.

"Damn, who the fuck is that, bro?" Bomani asked.

"Who?" Duke asked, turning around.

As soon as he turned around, I turned my head quickly, but I was caught. My heart started beating out of my chest.

"Pilar Renee," his sexy ass deep voice said.

I turned around like it was just a mistake that I had missed him.

"Yes, baby!" I grinned.

"Did you really think that you could walk by me and me not notice you. I've had my hands over every nook and cranny of that body. Don't play with me. Why are you dressed like this? Give me this fucking money," he spat, and then snatched all my little tips out my corset.

"Baron, tell Frank that he needs to get another girl out here while I go deal with this one in my office," he ordered.

He had my wrists so tight as he was dragging me through the place. I caught a glimpse of Mariah, Lee, and Swan, pointing and laughing. I was a little embarrassed. He pulled me in his office and slammed the door.

"Pilar, what the fuck you doing? This ain't no fucking strip club," he snapped, and threw my tips on the desk.

"Duke, all the other girls are dressed provocatively," I whined.

"You ain't all those other girls. You my fucking bitch. I don't give a fuck what them bitches wear."

"Oh, I'm your bitch."

I walked over and straddled him. I could feel his dick straining against his slacks. I grabbed his ears and started kissing him. I was biting all over his neck.

"Pilar, you better stop, for real," Duke moaned, latching on to my hair, and yanking my head back.

"Fuck me like I'm your bitch."

"Pilar, the way I'm feeling right now, I'll break your fucking cervix," he struggled to get out.

"Do it then," I whispered.

I wanted Duke to fuck me so hard. This man had been making love to me since I told him about my past. I get that he wanted to be gentle with me, but I need him to fuck me like his life was depending on it. I grabbed his throat and squeezed. He closed his eyes, leaning his head back on his seat. I let him go and stared at him. He freed his dick, laid me on his desk, and ripped my clothes off. He thrusted his dick in me so fast and hard. I grabbed his throat again, and he grabbed mine. He fucked me just like he said he would, like he was trying to break my fucking cervix.

He pulled out and flipped me over with no warning. He rammed his dick back in me, and damn near flipped my ass over the desk.

"Nah, bitch, this what you wanted. Take this fucking dick," he groaned.

He wrapped his hand in my hair like three times, pulling me back into his chest. I don't know what this nigga was touching, but 'in my guts' is a fucking understatement. He had my hair with his left hand, and grabbed my throat with his right.

"Ohhh shit, you like this shit, Pilar?" he grunted as he pumped inside me rapidly.

"I love it daddy, I love it," I managed to sputter out. "Choke me harder, bitch."

He did exactly what I said, and I was on the brink of passing out, but it felt so good. I couldn't stop him. I wouldn't stop him.

"You better make this pussy squirt, bitch. Make it squirt, or I'mma choke harder, and fucking harder. Squirt, Pilar."

As soon as he commanded me to squirt, my pussy squirted all over his dick. Every stroke after that, I squirted a little. This man had so much mind control over me, and he knew it.

"Shit, daddy finna cum in this lil' shit. You want daddy to cum?"

"Uhhhh huhhhhh," I moaned.

He gave me one long deep stroke, and I felt his warm liquids rushing inside of me. He let me go, and I fell over the desk. He fell back in his chair. I was literally trying to come back to earth. I was halfway dead.

"Pilar, your pussy leaking, baby. You better get it out my face, before I put my face in that shit. You know when I put my face in that pussy, my dick gon' get back hard."

I started making my ass clap. Duke spread my legs and stuck in his face in my pussy. He was eating my pussy so good.

"Twerk on this tongue, baby," he moaned, and slapped my ass.

Just as I was getting ready to cum again, someone bust through the door.

"Bro…what the fuck?"

Duke and I both jumped up. He quickly handed me his jacket so I could cover up. I rolled my eyes at the sight of Bakari's big headed ass.

"How the fuck are you in here fucking this bitch? So, did you have us off Blizz because he stole from your rich ass, or you wanted his bitch? Which one?" Bakari snapped. "You got all your people worried about if you over here dead or not. How long has this been going on? You haven't been home, and then your pre—"

"ENOUGH!" Duke yelled.

After that, they both went back and forth in their language. The only work I think I could pick up was the word bitch, and then Edwina. Duke told me that he would teach me Arabic soon, but he hasn't made an effort to yet. Duke got the very last word, and Bakari stomped out the door.

"Who's Edwina?" I asked.

"Huh? Who?"

"Who is Edwina? The name came up several times in that

argument. Who is she? I've asked three times, Duke, You're stalling."

"Nobody, Pilar. Seriously." He stared me in my eyes.

That stare always made me get butterflies in my stomach.

"Alright now, I hate to have to beat whoever she is, ass," I said rolling my neck.

"Baby, I can promise you, you are the only girl I'm worried about."

It was going to be awkward walking back downstairs with ripped clothing, so I told Duke to give me his button-down shirt. I put it on, and since it was tailored, it wasn't even that big on me. I gave him a kiss, and went back downstairs. Mariah, Swan, and Lee, were all sitting around the bar.

"Damn, girl, he fucked you out your clothes?" Lee asked.

I ignored her.

"Mariah, who is Edwina?" I asked.

One thing about me is when something is on my mind, it doesn't leave my mind until I'm satisfied with the answer. She looked at me like she had seen a ghost, which gave me an even more unsettling feeling.

"Who did Duke say she was?" she asked me.

"Mariah, I've learned that when you answer a question with a question, you're stalling. What is going on? Who is she?"

"Honestly, Pilar, I honestly cannot tell you any more than he has. Edwina is an old friend of his from back home. You don't have to worry about her. He is in love with you."

That answer didn't soothe me at all. Now, I'm going to be thinking about this Edwina person until I get a straightforward answer. All

I know is that it better add up to what the fuck these mothafuc saying, or I'mma do a one-eight-seven on they bitch asses.

"Okay, girl, just checking. I didn't want to have to beat nobc up," I said with a fake smile.

The rest of the night she looked nervous, but it was all good. I w going to get to the bottom of whoever this bitch is. If Duke is playi me, I swear to God, I was going to leave his ass and never talk to h again.

DUKE

*M*an, the more time I spend with this chick, the more I fall in love with her. In just a few short months, she has changed my life drastically. She got me volunteering with her ass on Saturdays. Charlie ass be there, and I be in between them. I haven't had time to check him out though. She got me going grocery shopping and shit. She even got me donating money. She told me that one of her dreams is to open up a home for homeless people. This girl got big dreams, and I'm going to be here to help her achieve each and every one of them.

It's funny because the same nigga I told Pilar I would never be to her, is the same nigga I'm being to my fiancée, Edwina. I can admit that I am deeply in love with Pilar, and I do not see myself being without her. I'm not going to leave her alone, but I have to do the right thing by Edwina as well. The crossroad I'm at now, is whether I want to leave Pilar to go be a father and the King, or I do I lose my crown, my fiancée and kid. I don't want to lose either one of them.

The argument between Bakari and I, was still on my mind heavily as I worked out in the gym. He basically told me that I was a piece of shit ass nigga, and not fit to be King. He told me that I was a piece of shit for leaving Edwina there alone, and that she thinks I haven't been to see her since she told me that she was pregnant. I had been having so much fun with Pilar that I hadn't even thought about home. I know it sounds terrible, but damn. Pilar also kind of pissed me off because she went behind my back and asked Mariah who Edwina was, but thankfully for me, she didn't open her mouth.

I was on my tenth mile when Mariah came in the gym. I slowed down to a slight jog to see what was going on.

"Duke, this is bad. Really bad," Mariah said, shaking her head.

"Mariah, I know. Damn! I fucked up," I spat.

"No, stupid ass, you did more than just fuck up," Mariah snapped back, while pressing the immediate stop button on the treadmill, almost making me break my leg. "Let me tell you what you did. You got an innocent girl's heart all into shit, and you *knew* that she could never be more than just a fuck to you. You fell in love, intentionally or unintentionally, I don't know, and now you stuck between a rock and a hard place. I told you from jump street to leave that girl alone. Now what you think is going to happen when you go back to Egypt and marry the mother of your child, huh?"

"Ugghhh," I groaned, swiping my hand down my face.

"You love her so much, but she doesn't even really know who you are. This life is all a lie. She doesn't know that you are Barak Ramses, the Prince, soon to be King. All she knows is Duke the Mogul. Duke, you foul, man. Real foul. I'm only mad because I have really grown to love Pilar like a little sister. I don't want to see her hurt, especially after everything that she has been through," Mariah said.

"I tried to tell him that," Baron said, walking into the gym. "His ass didn't listen. Now, guess what else? The King is pulling up in your driveway."

"Swear to God?" I asked.

"Bro, on everything. I took the shortcut over here so I could give you the heads up."

"Where is Pilar?" I asked no one in particular.

"She's still out with Swan and Lee. They went to go run bleachers at the Jaguars stadium. She's been gone for over an hour, which mean she is probably on her way back here now. I'll keep trying her phone," Mariah said.

"If you get her, tell her to stay at Swan's, and if you can't get her then fuck it." I shrugged.

The doorbell went off, and I knew who it was. I grabbed my sweat rag, and headed for the door. I opened the door, and the army of security men stormed in my house, and then the king.

"Well, hello, son. It's been a while," he said, shaking my hand. "I really like this place. Three of these things can fit into my house though. I'm sure there is somewhere that we can talk."

"King Dutch," Mariah stammered and curtsied.

"Mariah." He nodded at her. She scurried away quickly. "You been fucking her? She looks like she's getting thicker."

"No, Dad, we are just friends. That's all we have ever been, and all we will be. Please follow me."

We went into the den and took a seat. A few of his security guards came in behind us. Baron, Bomani, and Bakari also filed into the room. We stared at each other for a minute, before I broke the silence.

"So, what brings you all the way over here to the States?" I asked.

"Mariah, get me something strong to drink. On the rocks. The strongest thing in this house," he said, ignoring my question.

"Yes, sir."

"I just wanted to lay on eyes on you. I wanted to make sure you were okay because I hadn't seen you in months, whereas I'm used to seeing you every two weeks. Mrs. Ramses to be, seems to think that you have skipped out on your responsibilities. You know she is lugging around a big belly, and haven't seen the person responsible for it, in months. Care to explain?"

"Things have been real hectic over here lately. I just can't seem to find a free minute to get over there. Edwina knows it ain't nothing like that. I love her and my unborn."

Mariah came and set our drinks in front of us.

"You can't find a free minute, or you won't find a free minute? Before you answer that, I spoke with your little brother, Bakari, and he told me an entirely different story."

"And what story would that be, Bakari? I hope it was something along the lines of me being grown, and can do whatever the fuck I want to do." I cut my eyes at him.

"No need for hostility towards your brother. Does she know that she is nothing more than a piece of pussy, and that's all she ever will be. Does she even know your real—"

"Hey, daddy. What's going on? Is everything okay?" Pilar asked, walking into the room dripping in sweat.

She had on a Nike sports bra and compression shorts that had that ass sitting right. You could see the bottom of her damn butt cheeks. I was going to get on her ass for wearing that shit. I had to get her out of here fast, because I know my dad, and I know I my Pilar.

"Let daddy take care of some things, and I'll—" I started.

"The reason he can't find time to go see his family," Bakari said in our language.

We both cut our eyes at him at the same time.

"—Get with you later, mama," I finished my statement.

"Young lady, how did you get in here?" my dad asked.

Oh boy! I thought.

"I could ask you the same thing. My key is how I got in here," she said.

"Your key? You have a key?" my dad asked her, but was looking at me.

"Sure do," she nodded.

"If you knew who I was, you would lose that attitude before I have your little ass in the guillotine. Duke, you let this bitch talk to you like this?"

"Dad, don't do this. She doesn't know anything about this," I said to him in my language.

"Duke, I hope you are taking up for me while you speaking that yadda yadda shit to him. Is everybody in your fucking family disrespectful? Is that where that shit come from? This man looks like he's your father, so it is him who passed down being disrespectful to women. You should be ashamed of yourself. A woman is the very reason your black ass is here, and the nerve of your tacky ass to disrespect one. You disgust me," Pilar said rolling her neck.

My dad started to chuckle.

"Pilar, is it? I'm going to charge your little attitude to the game, because you really don't know who the fuck I am. So, if you don't mind, I would like to continue to have this conversation with my sons, alone, please."

She kissed me passionately and then bounced out the room.

"I didn't send you over here to forget your traditions. You do not, and I repeat do not let these bitches disrespect you. I don't know what's going on with that bitch you got, but you better end it. She's going to be heartbroken when she finds out that you can't marry her, nor produce with her."

"I'll figure that out six months from now."

"Correction, you're going to figure out in two weeks, because I have moved the engagement party up. You guys are going to be married before the baby is born. So, the engagement party is two weeks from now, and the wedding is going to be in three months, right before the baby is born."

"You come in here talking about traditions, but—" I started.

"I can change whatever rules that I want to change. You'll have that same privilege once you get your crown. *If* you get your crown."

"What you mean if? I worked my ass off, and busted my ass to get here. I don't think I follow you when you say *if*," I spat through gritted teeth.

"I say *if* because of that bitch that just left out of here. You are my first-born son. I know you. You are going to try and keep her around. I got a story that you had a nigga killed for that young tight pussy. You're sprung, but you better spring out of it. You got two weeks," he grinned and stood.

"Oh, and don't get any bright ideas, because if that bitch steps one foot in Egypt, she will be a dead bitch. I can't kill her over here, but over there, she's in my territory. I'll probably fuck that young pussy too, just to see why you're so sprung, before I choke the life out of her."

I jumped up, and his security guys trained their weapons on me.

"Whoa, whoa, whoa... Dad...Duke. Calm down." Baron stood up and got in between us.

"Well, well, well, look at him, bucking up at his father over his bitch. Two weeks, son," he said, patting me on my shoulder.

I followed him through the house and outside. Pilar was outside stretching. She was doing a handstand, and her legs were in a split. When she saw us, she flipped and got on her feet.

"I see why you sprung, son. That pussy looks like it can grip a dick good," my dad said to me in our language.

I wanted to react to my dad's vulgar statement, but I didn't want them to raise their guns at me again and have Pilar react. As soon as my dad was out the driveway, I yoked Bakari up in the tightest chokehold I could muster. Aware that Pilar was listening, I spoke Arabic.

"What was your angle, huh? What was your angle?" I rammed

his head into the wall.

"You don't deserve—" he sputtered out.

"And you do? You do? Give me one reason why you do."

"I'm more of a man than you will ever be."

I nodded my head and chuckled.

"Okay, MAN! Give me every credit card that I pay the statement on. Everything that I paid for, give it back, and make your own way MAN. You're fired. I'll send your last check to wherever you want me to send it."

When he slid to the ground, I grabbed his wallet out his pocket. I snatched his ID out and threw it on him.

"You're going to need that because from here on out, you're dead to me. I tried dealing with you, tried talking to you, but you're so headstrong that you can't even see how good you have had it, my nigga. But you are about to see now. If you think that your precious father is going to take care of you, then you will see.

Rainey, Romano, go lock his house up. Don't give him anything. He has all that he is going to need right there. HIS ID," I ordered them, and they scattered away.

"Matter of fact, let me give you your last check right now."

I pulled my wallet out, and threw two stacks on his chest. I got down and whispered in his ear.

"Breathe a word of this conversation, or anything regarding Edwina to Pilar, and I won't be so nice. Brother or not."

I patted him on his shoulder and told Pilar to come on. She

followed me in the house, and I could tell that she wanted to ask me what happened, but she didn't. We showered in separate rooms, because I just needed time to think. I wasn't going to leave Pilar. I knew that for sure, but I wanted my crown too. Fuck! I guess I have to do what I have to do.

PILAR

$\mathcal{F}$or the last two weeks, Duke had been acting strange as hell. I kept asking him to talk to me, but he told me that nothing was wrong. We even had been sleeping in separate rooms. He wouldn't touch me or anything. I guess it was because of his brother and his father. I don't know what they were saying, but I knew it was intense. I haven't seen Bakari since then. Hell, I hadn't even been seeing him in the pool hall. I was explaining everything to Swan and Lee in my room, as I packed my bags.

"Bitch, see, that's one reason why I couldn't date a mothafucka that speaks a different language than me. They probably be talking about how they gon' beat the fuck out of you," Lee said.

"I'm just happy that we get to go on vacation," Swan said, dancing.

Duke said that he had to go back home and take care of something. He told me that he would be back rather quickly, but I told him that I wanted to go, and I wasn't taking no for an answer. He told me that if I came, I was going to have to stay in the hotel because he supposed to come by himself. I told him that since I had to stay locked away then my girls better be able to come. Mariah was going anyway, because apparently, she had some things to take care of as well over there. We argued back and forth for a while until he gave in to me.

"Y'all ready?" Duke asked, stepping in the room.

"Yes," we said in unison.

"Damn, y'all. I swear we only going to be there for a couple of days, and y'all ass look like y'all have collectively packed a whole apartment."

"Whatever."

Romano and Rainey packed all of our things into the truck. I thought that we were going to a damn airport, but we went to an airstrip.

"Duke, you have your own jet?" I asked.

"Did you really think that I flew with hundreds of other people. God no! I need my space, and how could I put your little ass in the mile-high club if we are on the plane with a hundred people," he said and smiled.

I was happy as hell, because I hadn't had any of that good ass dick in two weeks. He was holding out on me. After we got on the plane, Duke told me that it was going to be a long one, so I might as well get comfortable. About two hours in, I fell asleep, and was awakened to Duke licking on my pussy. He was looking in my eyes, and I could tell that something was wrong with him. They weren't the same bright eyes that I was used to staring into.

"Duke, baby, tell me what's wrong?" I whispered.

I looked around, and everybody on the jet was sleeping. He hushed me, and continued to eat my pussy. He eats my pussy so fucking good every time, but this time, it felt different as hell. He was eating it with much more passion. He was eating it like it would be his last time eating it. He ate it so fucking slow, and with each stroke of his tongue, I was getting ready to lose it. He stuck two fingers in me, and stroked my g-spot with his long ass fingers. I nutted all over his fingers.

He leaned the seat back as far as it could go, and got on top of me. He placed his dick at my opening, and slid inside me. Placing my legs on his shoulders, he went deeper.

"Oh my goodnesss, daddy," I whispered.

"Pilar, you feel so fucking good to me, mama, fuckkk."

I don't know why I always get emotional when me and Duke make love, but when he strokes me long and deep, the tears come out of nowhere.

"Pilar, look at me. No matter what, I love you so much. I'm so in love with you. You have my heart, mind, body, and soul, baby. I promise you that," he whispered in my ear.

I grabbed the side of his face, looking him in his sad eyes, and pulled him towards my lips.

"I'm in love with you too, Duke. I'm giving you my mind, body, and soul. Promise me, you'll never hurt me."

He turned his head, and the tears instantly filled his eyes. He was biting his lip intensely as he slid in and out of me, slowly.

"Promise me, Duke."

"I promise, baby. No matter what, I'm in love with you, and you have my heart," he said, wiping my tears away.

"Fucccccckkk, baby, I'm getting ready to bust. You still ain't been taking that birth control?"

I shook my head and he smirked. He gave me another stroke, and I felt his dick pulsating inside me as he let off in me. After we got cleaned up, I laid on his chest. I can't believe that I'm actually in love with someone. I fell asleep with the biggest smile on my face.

"Baby, wake up." I was nudged.

I woke up as we were landing. It was so fucking beautiful, and absolutely nothing like what they show on TV. When I got off the jet, it felt so good over here. I was ready to go shopping though.

"Hey, baby! I'm going to head to my parents' house. You know I would invite you over, but I know you don't like my father, and I don't want to put you in an awkward position," Duke said, kissing on me.

"That's good, because I can't stand his extra mean ass," I spat, rolling my eyes.

"Alright, baby, there is no guarantee that I will see you—" he started.

"You make time for what you want to make time for. If you want to see me, then you will make time to see me. I know you have a lot of shit to do, so I forgive you already if I don't see you tonight."

"This is why you are the fucking best, mama. Romano and Rainey are going to take you to the hotel. Love you."

He kissed me, and I watched the car as they sped off. As we were on our way to the hotel, the sights over here was beautiful as fuck. I could see myself getting a vacation house over here or something to get away.

"Pilar, is Duke related to the King?" Lee asked.

"Nah, well, I don't know, why you ask?"

"The King's name is Barak Ramses. Duke's last name is Ramses."

"Could be. This place is only but so big. He doesn't really talk about his family much. Rainey, is Duke related to the King?"

"Umm, sure. You can say that," he responded.

I shrugged. We pulled up to the Hilton, and I fell in love instantly. We got settled in, and then searched the hotel for something to do. There was a spa in the hotel, so I paid for us all to get full body massages with Duke's credit card since he told me to do whatever I wanted to do in the hotel, as long as I didn't leave.

"Y'all, we have to do this more often. That massage was everything." Swan said as we were walking to the towards the room.

"Yo, Lari, what did you say that bitch name was? The one who kept coming up in the conversation between Duke and his brother?" Lee asked me. "Also, does Duke have a twin brother?"

"Edwina, why? No, he doesn't have a twin brother. I've met all of his brothers."

"Come look at this," Lee said.

I walked over to the flier that Lee was pointing at, and read the words.

Everyone is cordially invited to the engagement party of the Prince, Barak Ramses and Edwina Dubar.

The words didn't bother me as much as the photograph that was on the flier. It was a picture of Duke standing next to a very pregnant woman.

For his sake, he better have a twin...

TO BE CONTINUED

MESSAGE FROM AUTHORESS BIANCA

Hey, y'all! Thank you all so much for the love and constant support. When you get finish reading, please let me know how much you loved this book, with a review. It really means so much. As always, I have to thank God for blessing me with this talent that I never knew I had. I have to thank my P. Mae Sterling, for giving my talent the vision back in January of 2016. My Royalty sisters, I love you all so much for being such a constant support, and being such a strong group of women. Last, but certainly not least, I have to thank my readers. You guys give me the strength I need to continue to write. Reading your reviews and inbox messages make me feel so loved. Thank you for taking a chance on this new author.

With Love,

Bianca

CONNECT WITH ME ON SOCIAL MEDIA:

Facebook Readers Group: www.facebook.com/groups/AuthoressBianca/

Facebook Like Page: www.facebook.com/AuthoressBianca

Instagram: @AuthoressBianca

OTHER NOVELS BY BIANCA

www.amazon.com/author/bianca

Subscribe to my website: www.authoressbianca.com

Looking for a publishing home?

Royalty Publishing House, Where the Royals reside, is accepting submissions for writers in the urban fiction genre. If you're interested, submit the first 3-4 chapters with your synopsis to submissions@royaltypublishinghouse.com.

Check out our website for more information: www.royaltypublishinghouse.com.

Text ROYALTY to 42828 to join our mailing list!

To submit a manuscript for our review, email us at
submissions@royaltypublishinghouse.com

Text RPHCHRISTIAN to 22828 for our
CHRISTIAN ROMANCE novels!

Text RPHROMANCE to 22828 for our
INTERRACIAL ROMANCE novels!

Get LiT!

Download the LiT eReader app today and enjoy exclusive
content, free books, and more

Do You Like CELEBRITY GOSSIP?

Check Out QUEEN DYNASTY!
Visit Our Site: www.thequeendynasty.com

Made in the USA
Lexington, KY
06 March 2017